I WILL FIND YOU

THE EPIC STORY OF RJ AND YORK
BOOK TWO

SUSAN MAY WARREN

I WILL FIND YOU

I Will Find You

Of course the woman York loves has gone missing. He didn't know why he expected RJ not to chase danger into trouble. But she's in over her head, and he has to find her before criminal mastermind Alan Martin tracks her down.

RJ didn't mean to leave York behind, but she's on a mission to save a little girl caught in the crossfire of Martin's terrorist plot. Now, she'll have to find the girl and keep her safe while leaving clues for York to follow her.

But who will catch up to her first—York, or the man with a vendetta?

The gripping romantic adventure continues!

CHAPTER ONE

At least she hadn't been followed.

She thought.

Please.

RJ ducked into an alcove of a darkened pastry shop, the shadows hiding her, only her racing heartbeat to betray her, and waited.

Just like she'd seen York do in Paris a little over a week ago when she'd gotten them into this mess.

This terrible mess where now York lay recovering from a couple terrible stab wounds in a hospital in Italy. And she...

Well, she dodged in and out of shadows on the rain-soaked streets of Heidelberg, Germany, carrying a couple sandwiches in a greasy bag, taking a circuitous route back to where she'd left a ten-year-old, scared, little girl named Hana.

No one on her six, it seemed, even after ten long minutes, so she edged out. The air remained soggy after today's shower. Puddles pooled in the cracks of the narrow cobblestone streets in this area of old town, darkness pressing the windows of closed shops—souvenirs, cafes, gelato, pastries, jewelry stores and other tourist stops. The ruins of Schloss Heidelberg loomed over the old city like a giant, toppled and defeated, its craggy parapets and towers a testament to the protection once offered.

It was a city of romance, of history, and epic stories.

Of course, she was here, alone.

And on the run.

It seemed her M.O. of late.

She shivered, the early June air brisk under the now cloudless sky, and cool, after-rain wind. Probably, she should have grabbed a jacket for this so-called "quick trip" to Germany. *I'll be right back.*

The thought of her words to an unconscious York, the clink of her engagement ring landing on the stand beside his bed, the warnings shouting in the back of her mind only tightened her gut.

What. A. *Fool.*

The moonlight rippled on the waters of the Neckar River that threaded through the city. They'd spent the first night at a hotel across the old bridge, on the far banks of the river, a place that Ziggy had found them while she sorted everything out.

Ziggy had saved them, really, and RJ had never felt so far from the spy she wanted to be in the moment she'd realized she'd been betrayed.

By the one person she'd tried to save, of course, as all great stories went.

She came to the massive square, with the Gothic and Romanesque Church of the Holy Spirit rising from the center like a medieval specter. During the day, the square was a postcard—the mansard-roofed church with the cupola-topped steeple surrounded by storybook buildings. Red-roofed, with apartments over the ground-level shops, flowers spilling from sidewalk planters, and during the day, umbrella-topped cafe tables set up on the dark cobblestones near a number of quaint restaurants.

A place to linger, to ponder why she had this incessant ability to blow up all the good things in her life with an unquenchable need to fix, to help, to...rescue.

Movement from across the square had her stopping in the puddle of darkness beside the church. A couple, his arm around her shoulders, tucking her in tight.

RJ's chest tightened.

Please, York, still be alive.

She'd picked up a burner phone in Frankfurt when she'd landed, but her call to the Sigonella Air Base had been routed to the hospital switchboard, and the call to York's room went unanswered.

He was probably still unconscious after losing so much blood, and his traumatic surgery...yes, that had to be right because anything else had her shutting down, her thoughts careening together into a tight, inescapable knot.

But strange that Roy hadn't picked up—especially since this op was of his making. She wasn't exactly sure what Roy did for the Caleb Group, the clandestine private ops team that worked exclusively for American President Isaac White, but she had a guess.

One that gave him connections and resources around the globe.

The couple disappeared down a street and RJ took a breath, then braved herself out into the open, where the moonlight bathed the dark plaza, where anyone with a little heads-up knowledge and a little luck might center her in their sights and...

Well, and finish the job they'd started at KiTZ, the Hope Children's Cancer Center just down the road. Again, if it hadn't been for Ziggy—

She spotted the safe house just up the block, and three stories up, hidden in plain sight above an Indian restaurant called Raja's. Turning in under the hanging sign, she walked past the restaurant, now closed for the night, the smells of cardamom, cloves, ginger, and coriander saturated the red brick floor, the ancient waddle and daub walls.

The stairs creaked as she ascended. The second story opened to a terrace on the backside of the building with a view to the river, a door to their apartment to the right. She knocked, twice, waited, then knocked again, twice.

A lock clicked and the door opened.

A brunette opened the door, holding a small handgun. "You sure you weren't followed? You did everything I told you?"

RJ wanted to take offense as Ziggy's words, but frankly after everything that had happened over the past forty-eight hours, all she could do was nod. Hope.

She brushed past Ziggy, who shoved the tiny PDP Walther back into her belt, behind her.

"How's Hana?" RJ said as she walked into the tiny apartment. A small hallway led to two bedrooms, and a tiny bathroom with a skinny shower. The place *felt* like a safe house, clandestine and secret in the attic of a building.

"Sleeping." Ziggy said, but RJ checked for herself by going to the small bedroom with two single beds. Hana was a ball in the middle of the bed, her blonde hair shining under the light of the moon from the skylight window.

RJ nodded then turned to the kitchen. The lights were off—Ziggy's orders—but she knew it from the daylight. The place had sloping walls, and a window that cut into the mansard roof overlooked the building across the street. A small two-burner stove, a microwave, a micro fridge and a bare cupboard suggested that no one expected a long-term stay.

Ziggy leaned against the door frame to the kitchen.

Of course the spy who saved her was gorgeous. Long black hair, pulled back revealing regal cheekbones, piercing, golden-brown eyes, dusky light-brown skin. Lean and toned, she wore a pair of cargo pants, runners and a black tee-shirt that practically melded her into the night.

A female James Bond. Or maybe an actual Sydney Bristow.

That was a little slap in RJ's wanna-be confidence.

RJ looked like a tourist. Jeans, that she'd purchased at the airport, a white blouse, practically a neon glowing light, so again, very much *not* a spy.

No wonder Ziggy asked if she'd been spotted.

"Maybe you should have gone," RJ said, pulling out the sandwiches. "Liverwurst on rye, like you asked."

"And sauerkraut on the side. You used those words."

"I used those words. Here you go." She pulled out a to-go container of the fermented cabbage. "Gross. I got a cheese and ham for me. And pastrami for Hana." She pulled them out of the bag. "And this."

She handed a piece of paper to Ziggy who smiled. "Good job."

"What, is he your courier or something?"

"Or something." She read the note. "Okay. The safe house is ready for us."

"I thought this was the safe house."

"It belonged to a friend. Now his brother rents it out on Airbnb, but he lets me use it. In case of an emergency." She went over to a drawer, pulled out a matchbox, lit a match, then the paper and dropped it in the sink. "Let's wake Hana."

"We're going tonight?" She'd put the sandwiches on napkins. "Is Hana strong enough?" They'd pulled her out of a cancer ward, after all.

"Yes." Ziggy had a slight accent—RJ couldn't place it, but it sounded Italian, maybe. Or Greek. Which might be where she got her dark, exotic European look. "She doesn't have cancer."

A beat, and RJ frowned. "But —"

"Another one of Mad's lies," Ziggy said and took the sandwich from RJ. "Johan has the best liverwurst."

For a moment, RJ was back at the hospital, walking out with Hana in a wheelchair, the little girl confused but silent as her "father" fetched her from treatment—for her own safety.

RJ had thought herself a hero. Thought herself brave and crafty and smart, having outwitted Ruslan Gustov, a Russian scientist-slash-assassin, and Alan Martin, ex-CIA global terrorist. She'd gotten to Hana first—she and Mads—had rescued the little girl from being used as leverage.

Instead, they'd used her as bait. Because as she and Mads walked out under the cast of the late afternoon sun, a man had come up behind them and pressed a gun into her spine.

"Get in the van."

RJ's heart stopped on the voice of Alan Martin.

How—

Then, a van pulled up, doors opened.

She wasn't sure how it all went down behind her because suddenly Martin grunted, the gun left her spine and Mads, who RJ thought might reach for Hana to protect her, lit out for the van.

Leaving her and Hana on the sidewalk. RJ had grabbed the wheelchair and whirled around intending to run for the hospital.

Instead, she spotted Martin lying right there on the ground, bleeding from a gash on his temple, then glanced at the woman who'd felled him—she carried a crowbar—and froze.

"Roy sent me. C'mon." She gestured with her head, then took off.

It was then that Hana got up out of her chair, looked at RJ, and started to run.

So, not crippled, wasting away, about to die as Mads said.

RJ glanced over her shoulder at the van where she spotted Gustov, with his long blond hair, tall, imposing build—getting out.

Roger that.

She took off at a sprint, and noticed that Ziggy had grabbed Hana's hand, was pulling her along. Lights flickered on a late model 2-door BMW and Ziggy opened the door and practically shoved Hana in.

"Hurry up!"

RJ didn't look behind her, didn't think, just rounded the car and jumped in.

In moments, she was in a Bond movie, peeling out of the parking lot—reaching for the belt, of course, and making sure Hana was belted too—and winding through the streets of Heidelberg at high speed.

The car was sleek—black interior, stick shift, sunroof, and the woman at the wheel knew how to lose a tail.

They left the van after the second block and then spent the next two hours roaming the city, finally parking in an underground garage near the restaurant.

Hana had barely said anything, her green eyes rounded, her blonde hair breaking free of the braid that held it. She wore a pair of leggings and an over-sized shirt with Tweety Bird imprinted on the front, ballet slippers.

"Are you okay?" RJ asked when they finally got out. The sun had set, and she had no bars on her phone.

Hana had nodded, still wordless and frankly, RJ got it. She herself had no words for the way Ziggy had quick walked them to the apartment, then swept it—gun out—before she locked them inside. Disappeared.

RJ had called the hospital in Sicily for the first failed time.

Then she'd stood in the darkness, Hana curled on a sofa with a blanket over her, trying to unravel the mess she'd made of their lives and how it had all gone wrong.

Bottom line. She should have never left York.

Ziggy finally returned with rice and chicken from the restaurant on the first floor. They'd eaten in silence, Ziggy not offering anything in the way of an explanation.

And RJ hadn't any answers either, except the obvious.

Mads had betrayed her. But why? She'd rescued the scientist—twice.

Forty-eight hours later, she still hadn't pieced it all together. And now, "Hana really doesn't have cancer?"

Ziggy had taken a bottle of water from the fridge. "Nope. I tapped a friend who dug into the hospital records. Hana was there for observation only. And had been for about a month."

"Observation for what?"

"It isn't listed." Ziggy took a drink. "But my guess is that she was part of Mads' cover."

"He said he was her father. And that her mother had died—no, been killed in Paris. I even saw the body." She wouldn't long forget the gray corpse she'd watched fished out of the Seine. "Has she said anything?"

"Not a peep. She made a few origami animals from paper she found in a bookcase, then played with them for a while. I get the feeling she wasn't allowed out of her room much." Ziggy had taken her sandwich and brought it over to the table, sat down. "Poor kid. There is definitely something up with her, but she seems healthy."

"Could be shock. That first night, she slept with the covers over her head. I tried to talk to her, but she ignored me."

"Sometimes I feel like sleeping with the covers over my head," Ziggy said. Smiled.

RJ smiled back.

"So. According to Roy, you thought Mads had been kidnapped?"

"It's a long story, but yes. After Alan Martin escaped from prison, we spotted him in Paris where I then followed a known terrorist to a hotel. Watched him march Mads out of the building, and then I tracked them to a small hamlet about an hour away—one without Internet or cell service."

Ziggy wiped her mouth, her sandwich half eaten. "Why?"

"What why are you referring to? The why Mads was kidnapped? Or why the village, or even why did I think I could be some sort of hero and rescue him?" She shook her head, bringing her sandwich over to the table too. "Because that's who I am—I leap before I look, and I get people in trouble, and maybe I am running from something like Giselle said, and I can't believe I left York in Italy, fighting for his life, and even worse I took off his ring and told him something stupid like I'd be right back to get it, when in fact, I'm stuck here in Germany, on the lam from international terrorists, eating a cold dinner with...well, as much as I appreciate everything you did, I don't know you and...." She put the sandwich down. "I just don't understand why Mads betrayed us."

"Okay, that covers a lot of it," Ziggy said. "And, to your question, I work, sometimes, with Roy, and he asked me to meet you at the hospital. I saw what was going down as soon as I spotted you—Roy gave me a pretty good description of you, and it wasn't hard to figure out that you were in trouble, the way that man came up to you. The rest was instinct."

"Does Roy know where we are?"

"He will. My phone died, but...he will find us."

She didn't know how. "I need to pick up a burner phone."

"He will find us."

RJ sighed. Took a bite of her sandwich. European bread could make her eyes roll back into her head.

"Who is Giselle?"

RJ wiped her mouth. Took a sip of her own bottled water. "A wise Uber driver from Paris who said that I was running from wanting to be a wife and mother."

Ziggy raised a dark eyebrow.

"York took me to Paris about a week ago to propose. Which he did. And I said yes. But now I'm thinking—what if I subconsciously didn't mean it? I mean, I did leave his ring behind."

"Why?"

"I don't know."

Ziggy nodded, looked out the window past her. "You were the one who stopped the assassination of that Russian General."

She looked at her then, stilled.

"We all heard about it. Brave."

"Or stupid."

"Might have stopped a war."

"Nearly got myself and my brother killed. Not to mention York."

"York knows how to stay alive."

Her comment lodged inside RJ. Yes. Yes, he did.

But how did this woman know that?

Maybe she read RJ's mind because she smiled. "I've never met him, but he's a bit of a legend."

Huh.

"I never really introduced myself. Ziggy Mattucci."

"RJ Marshall. Are you CIA?"

She laughed. "Never. You?"

"In a different life."

"Not so different from this one."

"I was an analyst."

"Oh. So maybe a little different." She winked.

"Thanks for what you did. I don't know what would have happened if you hadn't shown up."

"I'm sure you would have" — She stilled, looked past RJ. Then — "Get down!"

She leaped for RJ just as the window shattered behind her.

"You shouldn't have let her go alone."

York wasn't sure who, exactly, he was talking to—Roy, or himself—as they exited the rental car and crossed the street to *Schlemmer-Markt*, a tiny, semi-lit deli with thick blocks of gourmet cheese and hanging sausages in the window. A hush fell over the streets, the twilight already dissolved into the moon swept river. The air hinted of the earlier rain, still dour, looming, and it only made York's insides ache.

Then again, he was two days out of a nearly lethal stabbing, blood loss, and emergency surgery, so maybe it wasn't the rain. Or *just* the rain.

Or maybe the ache was deeper, in his bones, in his heart.

RJ had left him.

Left. Him. Ring on the nightstand in his hospital room, left him. And sure, he had a deep and faint memory of her voice saying, "I'll be right back," but then again, maybe he simply hoped it.

Maybe, instead, her desire to do more, *be* more, live bolder and wilder had finally taken over and pushed her permanently out of his arms.

Out of the life he'd hoped for them.

"Hindsight," Roy growled. He wore his signature black—black jeans, black shirt, black jacket, black countenance. The man had grim and lethal oozing out of him, and it had only gotten worse as their hunt for RJ over the past twenty-four hours turned up empty.

They crossed the street and Roy opened the door to the deli.

"Not real hungry."

Roy just grunted. York followed him as he headed up the counter, past a couple tables, occupied with people plugged into their cell phones, a woman and her son eating sandwiches, a couple sharing a pizza. The scent of fresh bread, thyme, rosemary, sausage and frothy beer pulled him in and awakened a hollowness inside him.

Maybe he might be a little hungry.

But how could he think of food when the woman he loved —and he'd always love RJ, despite their dismal ending—could be hurt, or kidnapped or…

Or maybe just, finally, ditching him.

"I need to speak to Johan," Roy said to a woman at the counter. He said it in German, but York knew enough to understand it. His clandestine years swooping in to save the day.

He'd probably never really escaped them. Just tucked them into his back pocket while he desperately tried to be someone else. Mack Jones, local burger flipper, bartender, bouncer.

A guy who wanted a regular life. A family.

He'd seen the dream fade hard yesterday when he'd woken in an Italian hospital to the news that RJ had not only gone to Germany without him, to rescue the daughter of a scientist wanted by two terrorists at the least, and maybe an entire country—aka Russia—at the worst, but that RJ, along with said scientist, was missing.

He had put on pants, slipped the ring into his pocket, and grabbed a bite on the plane that his boss, Logan Thorne, director of the Caleb Group, had provided a few hours later. His appetite had vanished, however, when they'd arrived at the hospital, procured the CCTV tapes and glimpsed a small throw down in the hospital parking lot.

"She's with Ziggy. I'm sure of it," Roy said now as the woman he'd talked to disappeared into the back of the restaurant, probably the kitchen.

"The same Ziggy that you've tried to call a dozen times?" York's mouth tightened around the edges, probably what elicited Roy's sigh.

"I don't know why she's not answering, but we'll find her."

"How do you —"

Roy held up his hand and turned as a man emerged from the back. Burly, dark-blond hair, brown mustache, he wore an apron but reached out a beefy hand over the counter that could crush a windpipe. "Roy."

"Johan." He glanced at York, gestured at him with his chin. "He's one of ours. York Newgate."

Johan lifted an eyebrow. "I have heard of him."

York drew in a breath, hoping he hadn't translated the man's words correctly. He'd spent the last three years trying to dodge the man he'd been.

Then again, it just might be that man who could find RJ and get her out of this mess.

"Have you heard from Ziggy?" Roy asked.

"Liverwurst on rye, sauerkraut on the side." He reached under the counter and pulled out piece of paper, scratching an address on it. "An hour ago, maybe more."

Roy took it between his pointer and index finger. "Danke."

Johan reached into the glass case and pulled out a sandwich on sourdough bread. "For your friend." He wrapped it in paper, then handed it to Roy.

He gave it to York on the way out. "You're looking pretty gray. You might need a nap."

York had managed a couple pain pills on the plane, but they may have worn off. "I'll worry about sleeping after we find RJ." He opened the sandwich. "What is this?"

"Liverwurst. It's good. And this —" he handed York the paper. "Is the address where they're staying."

The relief simply turned him weak, sweeping through him, rattling his bones. He slid into the passenger seat and took a full breath.

"Hurry."

"We need to make sure we weren't tailed." Roy pulled out in the rental, a mid-sized sedan without any *oomph* and took to the street slowly. York glanced out the side mirror as he ate the sandwich.

The liver pâté, sourdough, red onions and mayo went down fast and easy.

"Streets are barren."

Roy grunted again.

"What I can't figure out is how Alan Martin knew she was there," York said.

Silence on the driver's side suggested either Roy was as confused as York or—

"What aren't you telling me?"

Roy turned onto a side street, darkened by the lack of streetlights, then again on the next street. "I'm just going back to that moment when she spotted Martin right outside the coffee shop where she happened to end up for her morning brew. Coincidence, much?"

That had been bothering him, too.

"And then there's Ruslan Gustov."

The name turned his gut to a knot. He crumpled the empty sandwich wrapper in a fist.

"The brother of the assassin who chased you across Russia, to America, and nearly killed you —"

"And RJ."

"Right. Not to mention your girlfriend in Russia, and… sorry, York, but I have to say it—your wife and son."

The words didn't hurt as much anymore. Still, he felt them, a thumb in his wound. "I'm not sure it was him. Could have been Martin. Or any other member of the Bratva, trying to send me a message."

"Right. Still, what is Ruslan— a scientist—doing trying to grab RJ from a parking lot outside a children's hospital in Heidelberg, Germany?"

So many good questions. "I'm thinking he's not a scientist anymore."

"Or he's added skills to his job description."

"And how did they find them?"

Roy took another turn. "You saw the video. Mads ran toward the van. Left his daughter behind—which makes me wonder if she is his daughter. My gut says that Mads lured RJ to Germany, set her up."

"She rescued him after they kidnapped him. Why would he run *to* them?"

"I think we need to put in a call to Coco and see what she can dig up on him. Do some surfing on the dark web."

He'd already been in contact with the Caleb Group stateside hacker in hopes that RJ would contact her sister. So far, nothing.

Please, RJ, phone home.

"The good news is that it looks like RJ and Ziggy got away from them. For now." Roy pointed to the paper, now shoved in the dash cubby.

"What's this address? A safe house?"

"Not really. Apartment. Used to be owned by his brother. Now Johan rents it as an Airbnb. No wonder Ziggy went there."

"Who is this woman, Ziggy?"

Roy glanced at him. "You know her. Or *of* her—code name Tiger sound familiar?"

The name shifted through him, locked in place. "German. Black ops. Rumor has it she was captured."

"Escaped. She's a freelancer now."

There were other adjectives for her circling through the clandestine community—sexy, calculating, lethal.

"She's a friend," Roy said, as if to put to bed the questions in York's mind. "She'll keep RJ safe. I promise."

His words only raised more questions. But Roy said nothing more, his face barely illuminated by the dash lights.

"Did Logan say anything more about the flight we managed to save?"

As if on cue, his back began to hurt, and for a moment, he was watching the glow of flames upon the dark waters of the Ionian Sea, a *hoo-rah* rising through him at seeing the EMP bomb that had been aimed at a commercial jet sink into the sea.

Then, of course, Martin had surprised him with a blade to the back, then a second stab with a twist, chewing up his insides.

He would have sunk to the bottom of the sea, along with the boat he'd destroyed, if it hadn't been for RJ and Roy finding him in the water.

"Like I said, all doctors and researchers from various African countries. She did discover that they were en-route to a medical conference in Florence and had scheduled to meet the new CDC director—Landon Grey. He just took over a couple weeks ago."

"What happened to the previous director?"

"Car accident." Roy turned again and headed over the bridge. The moon dappled the water. Ahead, the hulking mass of the ruined Heidelberg castle overlooked the village below the cliffs.

I'm on my way, RJ. Please stay put.

"Any idea what they were meeting with him about?"

Roy touched the brakes as he came up on a driver of a scooter. "He was at the base checking on quarantine protocols since they're the first stop out of Africa or the Middle East for our soldiers. Maybe they were giving him updates on the current viruses coming out of Africa. He is headed to the Florence conference too, according to Coco."

The scooter turned off and Roy slowed as they approached old town, with the narrow, cobbled streets, the ancient buildings, with darkened shops at the base and apartments with lights glowing out from closed blinds above.

Yes, it would make a decent place for an Airbnb.

And his brain just found its way back to the hotel room in Paris, the one he'd rented with the hopes of proposing in a restaurant in the Eiffel tower. A reservation that got trampled on by one superstar, arrogant, wanna-be spy actor named Winchester Marshall who, yes, also happened to be RJ's cousin.

Who really, after all, started this entire mess when he got them ousted from the hotel coffee shop.

Which brought York right back to— "Yes, why was Martin standing outside the coffee shop that RJ just happened to be at? Especially since twenty-four hours earlier, he was busy escaping custody in Virginia?"

Roy stopped at the end of a street, beside a gelato shop. Next to it a video store offering dubbed American movies.

"And how did he find her, if he was there for her?" Roy turned off the car.

And York's brain stopped on a poster in the window of the video store. Winchester Marshall, dressed in a tuxedo, leaning against a sports car.

Jack Powers, international spy, to the rescue.

What an arrogant—

"Winchester Marshall is her cousin." The words emerged quietly, just his thoughts, audible.

Roy glanced at him, frowned. "So?"

York looked at him, his brain reaching for pieces. "You know, an actor has all sorts of perks that regular people don't have. They can get backstage. They can hire security to protect them. They can travel internationally, and meet with dignitaries who are fans and..."

Roy gave him a look.

"What if Marshall is...I don't know—working for the CIA. The rogue group."

"Like Frank Sinatra."

"Sinatra worked for the CIA?"

"There are rumors—some of them debunked—that he was a dispatcher—flew people secretly in and out of the country on his private jet."

"That sneak. Actually, I was thinking John Wayne," York said. "He allegedly spied for the OSS during USO tours."

"Cary Grant did some spying too—for the Brits."

"Exactly. The government has a history of using famous people—actors, athletes, political figures—for their own purposes. What if Marshall is working for Martin?"

Roy's hand had stopped on the door handle. "But how did Winchester Marshall know he'd see RJ in Paris? It's a pretty big what-if."

"He's a Marshall. You've met them, they seem to pop up everywhere."

Roy's mouth ticked up one side. "Right. Well, if we ever seen him again, we'll ask."

Yeah he would. But yes, with Roy's question, the theory felt reaching.

His brain just longed to untangle it all, maybe.

He grabbed the door handle. "What a mess. I just wanted to go to Paris. Get engaged. Marry the woman I love. Start a new life."

"And leave this one behind."

York nodded, glanced at Roy. "Don't you...ever want to start over? Leave? Live...I don't know, a life where your biggest problem is getting the mower to start?"

Roy smiled, something sad. "That's why I like you, York."

He frowned.

"You still believe that's out there." He pushed open the door. "Let's get RJ."

The smells of coriander, curry and pepper scented the air as York followed Roy down the street. A sign hung over the entrance to an Indian restaurant, the lights glowing out of the front window. Roy went inside, passed the restaurant entrance and headed to the door in back, the one that led to the apartments upstairs.

They took the two flights in silence, the ancient stairs squeaking. If they ever decided to turn it into a safe house, they had a built-in security system.

Roy rounded the landing for the last run of stairs then stilled. Reached for his gun, secured in a holster under his jacket.

York felt a little naked.

"Door's ajar," he said and held up his hand in a fist.

Stop.

Fine. He let Roy, the man with the weapon, go first as he crept up to the apartment on the top floor. To his left, another door—also ajar—went out to a broad rooftop terrace. In the distance, the river turned silver in the starlight.

Roy edged the door open, then rolled in, his gun out. He flicked on the light.

"Clear," he said, and York followed him in.

Roy checked the kitchen, then went to the bedrooms, maybe even the bathroom. He came back. "Empty."

York stood in the kitchen, his breath a razor in his lungs. Glass shards glinted off the light from a hole in the windowpane. A tiny round table lay toppled on its side, a chair turned over, another one also taken down. A couple sandwiches, not unlike the one he'd just eaten, were tossed across the room—bread, salami, lettuce.

And on the floor, near the table, the chairs, the glass... blood. It pooled, rusty, then smeared across the yellow floor tiles. A handprint pressed the counter, and a smudged footprint lead out to the carpeted hallway.

He followed it. It faded into the bedroom, near the small twin bed, and from there, vanished.

But he could do the math.

"Someone was shot," Roy said, coming into the room.

York looked at him. *"Really?"*

Roy held up his hands. "I'm just the messenger. The blood isn't entirely dry, but it's darkening. I'd say maybe an hour, at most."

York's gut wanted to lose the liverwurst.

He walked past Roy, back out into the hallway. Stared down the stairs.

Then looked out, onto the terrace.

The door still hung ajar.

He pushed it open and walked out into the darkness. A table, a couple chairs. And along the edge, a skinny metal staircase that probably served as a fire escape led to the ground, some three stories below.

Leaning over the side, he hoped—terribly, brutally—he'd find RJ hiding in the bushes of the courtyard. But the space was empty, save for a dumpster, an old bike and a dog sniffing at a bush.

It lifted its leg and York turned away.

"Anything?" Roy, behind him.

York shook his head, stared out toward the river, the city that spanned the far side of the river, with its quaint red roofs and cobblestone streets. Romantic. Epic.

And the woman he loved was out there, without him. Possibly hurt. Possibly even being tortured and killed by the men who hunted him.

Still.

He leaned on the ledge, breathing hard.

"Hey, York—you okay?"

Not even a little. But he would be. He had to be.

He drew in a breath. Stood up. "You're not the only one with friends, Roy. It's time to do things my way."

Then he turned and headed back down the stairs.

CHAPTER TWO

Time to stop kidding herself.

This wasn't a game. Wasn't fun. Wasn't even an adventure.

This was real stakes, real bullets.

Real blood.

RJ just wanted to get off the train.

And not just the imagined one where people were trying to kill her, but the actual one that now carted Ziggy, Hana and herself to parts unknown.

At least to RJ. Ziggy seemed to know exactly where they were going. She sat across from RJ on a bench, trying to ease her jacket from her bloodied arm, where only three hours ago, she'd saved RJ's life.

Tackled her onto the kitchen floor, catching the bullet meant for RJ's head, probably, leaving a terrible gash across her upper arm.

It had bled fast and profusely, Ziggy's hand over it as they'd scrambled out of the apartment. RJ still couldn't remember scooping up Hana, or even grabbing a towel for Ziggy's wound, but somehow, she did both. Even tied the towel around Ziggy's arm as she fought with the fire escape off the balcony.

"The stairs might only lead to an ambush," she'd said as the stairway dropped.

Yep. RJ had done that math, too.

Hana had climbed down without a word, without fear in her eyes, and without a sound.

Which made RJ wonder just exactly who this little girl was, and what she harbored behind those big blue eyes and closed mouth.

She now sat on the train bench, her knees pulled up to her chest, her arms around them, staring out the window at the black night, the shapes of silver-tipped pine trees cascading past the window.

"Let me help," RJ said and grabbed the end of Ziggy's jacket arm, holding it so she could shrug out of it. Only the slightest narrowing of her eyes, the tightening of her jaw evidenced pain. She'd ditched the bloody towel at the train station and had pulled on the jacket to conceal the wound in the bathroom, out of her backpack.

RJ had grabbed her backpack too, but only because Ziggy had practically thrown it at her on their way out of the flat.

The wound had stopped bleeding, mostly, dark blood caked into Ziggy's shirt. She eased up the cuff to take a better look, closed one eye as the fabric tugged on the dried blood.

RJ got up and sat beside her. "Let me." Then she opened her bag and pulled out a bottle of water. Took a towel hanging in their train compartment and wetted the wound, catching the water.

"How did you know —"

"I saw the gun—or what I thought might be the gun—just a spark of light through the window, but, instincts."

RJ loosened the shirt and rolled it up. The wound was

jagged, at least a thumb's depth and width. It needed stitches—maybe six or ten of them. "We should have grabbed first aid supplies —"

"I have superglue in my pack."

RJ raised an eyebrow.

"It's better than stitches. And besides—everything was closed. We're lucky we got a train."

Ziggy had led them right to the train station, scoured the board and bought tickets on the only outgoing train—to Vienna, Austria.

"Where are we going? Just anywhere?"

Ziggy had zipped open the front pouch of her pack and pulled out a used bottle of superglue.

"Seriously."

"Just pinch the edges together and seal it. It'll heal. And no, not anywhere. We're going to my home. It's safe."

RJ opened the container, set the top on the table between the seats, and then pinched together the wound, starting at one end. She applied the glue as she went, sealing it shut.

"We need antibiotics or something."

"I'll be fine." She pulled out a roll of duct tape. "Bandage."

"You're just like my father," RJ said as she sealed the wound. "He'd be out in the field, get cut by barbed wire or nicked by a cow's horn and he'd pull out the duct tape."

"You grew up on a farm?"

"Ranch. In Montana." She smoothed the tape over Ziggy's wound. "You?"

"Italy. On a vineyard near a little town outside Florence called Lucca."

"You were raised on a vineyard?"

"Not so different from a ranch—a life dependent on the weather, the soil, hard work." She leaned back on the seat and closed her eyes. "I miss it."

A beat, and Ziggy opened her eyes. "Don't you miss home?"

"I...I miss my family, sometimes, but no. I couldn't wait to leave the ranch. Do something big with my life. I joined the CIA out of college and became an analyst."

"But you wanted to be a spy." Ziggy's mouth tweaked up one side.

RJ lifted a shoulder. "Maybe. I guess so."

"And now?"

RJ moved back over to her seat. Glanced at Hana. She had leaned against the wall, her braids a mess. RJ should have grabbed that sandwich for her. Now, she reached into her bag and found an apple she picked up at the airport.

"Hungry?"

Hana glanced at her, then the apple. Then back to RJ. Took a breath.

RJ moved it closer to her.

Hana took it, and then, holding it with both hands, dug in.

"I don't know," RJ said to Ziggy's question. "Right now, I just want to find York and go home."

The wind blew against the train, the clacking of the wheels rhythmic and hypnotic. The last time she'd been on a train, it had been with York, during their escape through Russia.

"He'll find us," Ziggy said. "Trust me. If York is anything like his reputation, he'll find us."

RJ frowned. "What is his reputation?"

"It's just...well, they called him the Bird back when I was getting started. Not sure why, but some said because he was able to be everywhere. He just sort of showed up, right time, right place."

RJ nodded. "He rescued me from being shot during an assassination attempt on a Russian General. Just - grabbed me right off the street. Kept me safe, got me out of the country."

"He was a real Bond. At the top of his game when he met you, RJ."

"And now he wants to settle down, start a family. Honestly, I didn't believe it the first time he said it. He lost his memory a couple years ago, and got a taste of that life, but when it all came back to him, I thought he'd put it behind him. But now, maybe, I get it."

"Nothing like an attempt on your life to make you want to hang up your gun."

"I don't have a gun. I learned how to shoot on the ranch—a little. But really, I have no training. Not in weapons, or hand-to-hand combat, or spycraft. I'm just...I'm just a normal person with a terrible ability to get in over my head."

Ziggy pulled up her jacket and wadded it into a ball, then shoved it behind her neck, leaning against the window, away from her injured arm. "You don't have to have special skills to be a hero. You just have to do what's right, despite the cost." She closed her eyes. "My great-grandfather taught me that. If it weren't for his weaknesses, I wouldn't even be here."

"I thought you said he was a hero."

"He was. Didn't mean he didn't make mistakes."

Hana had finished the apple, had eaten it all the way down to the core, and then that, too.

Now, she lay on the bench, her knees to her chest, her head on her hands. Poor thing. RJ reached for the blanket on the top bunk and pulled it down. Then she spread it over the little girl.

Her eyes opened a moment, and she considered RJ.

Then, she flashed a smile, just one side of her mouth and pulled up the blanket.

It was gone in a moment, and she closed her eyes.

RJ scooted back on the bench, her back against the wall. "So why do you call him a hero?"

"It's a long story."

Right. And it was late. And Ziggy was hurt and tired—

"I was named after him."

She glanced over at Ziggy. Her eyes were closed, but maybe her wound was keeping her awake. "Oh?"

"Sigfrida. It's a family name, after Sigfrid, but he called himself Fred."

"Fred."

"Jones. Fred Jones. From Minnesota."

"He was American?"

"Infantry. With the 92nd division. He was a scout. Fought in the siege of Lucca, "

"Wait. He was an American soldier?"

"Mmmhmm." Ziggy repositioned her jacket. "I still remember my great-grandmother telling me the story. And he wasn't the only warrior. She was only eighteen at the time of the German occupation, but even then, she was a partisan. It was just in her Italian blood. She was feisty, all the way to the end. Thick white hair, her leathery skin. She'd walk the vines every day, working with the grounds keeper to prune them, taking off leaves to help the sun find the right grapes. It's her recipe that they still use on the farm to make the wines."

"What happened to your great-grandfather?"

"Oh, he died long before I met him. But she could make him come alive. Golden-brown eyes—that's why I got his name, I think. And a laugh that she said turned her from broken to living. She said the day she found him, asleep in the vines, bloody and near death was the day God saved her life."

"Why was he near death?"

"He'd been scouting behind enemy lines, in preparation for the Allied invasion. It was about eight months since D-Day, and the Allies were routing Germany back into Europe, so they sent troops to the shores of Italy. Mostly to distract and weaken the Germans, but we were fighting our own war, here, and they came to help. A real civil war—most of the country didn't want Mussolini and his fascists, and many of the youth had risen up as partigiano—resistance fighters. My Nonna was one of them. She used to ride her bike between hilltop cities, messages stuffed in her shoes, as a courier. Right past German or Italian guards. Told me it was terrifying, but after the death of her father, she couldn't sit still and do nothing."

"Your great-great grandfather."

"Yes. He was a resistance fighter, too, but had been captured, early on, and hung in the square in their town. Her mother broke, and Nonna—her name was Angelica—took over raising her little brother and running the vineyard. But as the Germans took over their lives, she knew she couldn't sit still. A colonel had even taken up shelter in her home, in her father's room and that's what started it. She learned German—Nonna was smart as a whip—and would record their conversations, pass it on to local fighters."

"And she never got caught?"

"Oh, she got caught. But that's another story." Ziggy opened her eyes and smiled. "We were talking about Fred."

"Fred. Bloody. Alone in a field."

"His platoon of scouts had stumbled upon a group of German soldiers. Everyone scattered. He was shot but managed to get away. Ran through the night, finally dropped in a field, and that's where Nonna found him —"

"Bloody and near death."

"She put him in a wagon, dragged him up to the house and hid him in the wine cave, behind the barrels while she nursed him back to life."

"Feels like a war romance."

Ziggy smiled. "How do you think I got here." She sighed. "Fact is, all great love stories involve pain and sacrifice. But that's what make them so epic, right?"

Her eyes closed. "You'll have your happy ending, RJ. I'm sure of it. I'm just not sure how we'll get there." She put her jacket on the bench, lifted her legs and lay down. "Go to sleep. Tomorrow will look better."

RJ stared out the window, the world gray and blurry.

And tried to believe.

Berlin, Germany

"You sure this is a good idea?"

Roy voiced York's thoughts as they sat at a picnic table in the *Prater Bier Garten*, deep in the heart of Berlin.

Not even a little. But York was running out of leads, choices and even hope twenty-four hours after he stared out into the dark night in Heidelberg, so, "It's all I got."

York had no appetite. Maybe it was the pain, slowly encasing his body after their travel from Berlin on a day train. Or, the fact he had no time, no focus to eat—not with his gaze on the crowd packed into the massive outdoor beer hall, twinkle lights glowing from massive strands that stretched across the open-air grounds. From the stage on the far end, a post-punk indie band screamed out a mess about despair, anger and frustration, with a cacophony of metal and drums that roiled into the night.

It seemed an appropriate soundtrack to this meet and greet.

"And you trust this guy?" Across from him, Roy nursed a bratwurst and fries, which went well with his frothy glass of deep-brown Prater Schwarzbier.

Roy was younger than him by a good five years, had a head of dark hair, no scars on his face—not yet, and was built like the SEAL he'd been. He defined dark and grim and the kind of guy you wanted with you when you walked into an alley. Or at a beer park with a known former Russian gangster.

Overhead, the sky had turned deep indigo, the air balmy. Wind reaped the fragrance of nearby linden trees, pots filled with geraniums, and the fried schnitzel from the nearby restaurant. The quaint community of red-roofed apartment buildings, rose around them, and inside the garden, families sat at the tables, jammed together, laughing, eating pretzels and pickles and boiled potatoes.

"Not even a little," York said. "But if anyone knows where RJ might be—and if Martin has her, it's Gregori Dumas."

"Ex-FSB?"

"Ex-everything. Used to run with the Petrov Bratva. Probably still does, although he's connected to everyone—the thirty-six Boys from Germany, the Camorra, the Roma gangs, even the Pink Panthers, ex-Yugoslavs who specialize in diamond heists."

"And he's what to you?" Roy asked, picking up a thick waffle fry.

"He owes me." York scanned the crowd one last time for the pocked-faced man, about six-two, lean and grim, a scar that ran across his cheek. A real ladies man.

Except York had his own scar, from a bombing once upon a time, and frankly, different time, different place, he might be exactly who Gregori had turned out to be.

If not for RJ, really, who'd appeared in his life, a light that yes, he'd had to save, but in the end, she'd save him, over and over.

Mostly from himself. And the man he no longer wanted to be.

Until now.

"You should eat," Roy said, indicating his untouched

wiener schnitzel and bottled water. "Especially if you're expecting to go on an impromptu field trip with this guy."

"I just need him to listen. Maybe ask a few questions."

"You're not planning on getting a tattoo and taking any brotherhood oaths, are you?"

York had been watching a man with a woman, a little girl on his shoulders as they found a table. The man pulled the little girl down and tickled her before setting her on what York assumed was his wife's lap.

He looked at Roy. "Not if I can help it."

Roy set down his beer. "I was kidding."

"If Martin has her, then...I'm getting her back, Roy."

He met Roy's gaze, even when Roy drew in a breath. "I see. And if it's you in exchange for RJ?"

He said nothing.

"Can you trust this guy?"

York twisted the top off his water bottle. "No. But like I said, he owes me."

"How?"

"I got his wife out of Russia, back when I was in the transportation business." He took a drink. Capped the bottle.

"That's what they called it?" Roy said.

"Just like you're in the information business."

Roy nodded, picked up a fry. "I prefer professional tourist."

York winced, the wound in his back still a deep, persistent throb. He might even be running a fever.

He'd changed clothes at the cheap hotel just a few blocks from here, re-taped his wound—it looked pretty red, fairly swollen in the mirror—added a jacket and his Ka-Bar to his belt.

Now, it dug into his side.

At least he was out of his sodden, wrecked clothing from three nights ago. Although he'd picked up his suitcase—and

RJ's for that matter—from the hotel where they'd been staying at in Catania, Sicily, he hadn't taken time to change.

Mostly because he'd been momentarily overwhelmed with his stupidity, the memories of his words to RJ right before he'd walked away from the woman he loved.

Maybe this was exactly where he was supposed to end up—RJ ripped from him, the life he'd tried to escape clawing him back in. York had clearly been lying to himself when he thought he could leave it behind, start over.

No. He was destined to live with a shadow over his shoulder.

A man emerged from a cluster of tattooed, pierced, purple-haired youth, dancing and jumping as they listened to the band. He worked his way through them, protecting his beer.

Gregori Dumas.

York nearly didn't recognize the former KGB interrogator-slash-defector-mafia thug. Life had added layers to Gregori's waist, a jowl under his chin, whitened his hair. Made him softer, maybe a little more godfather in his appearance.

All he needed was a cat.

Gregori spotted York—probably had been scoping him out for hours—nodded, then took a circuitous route toward him, his gaze falling on a couple skirts on his way toward them.

"He's here," York said.

Roy pushed his food away. "Okay. Here's what's going to happen." He picked up a napkin. "You talk, I'll keep an eye out for friends. But you don't go anywhere without me."

York frowned at him.

Roy frowned back. "RJ is alive. And I'm not going to be the one to tell her that the man she loves vanished into the Bratva."

"I'm not going to vanish into the Bratva." Yet. Although...

He got up and held out his hand to Gregori. "*Zdrastvootya.*"

"*Voron,*" Gregori said.

His old name—the Bird. Or Raven, as they called him in Russia.

Roy had retrieved his food, kept his head down, as if not listening.

York switched to Russian. Not to keep Roy out of the loop—probably the man knew the language well enough. But it kept the conversation easy, without hiccups in translation. "Thanks for meeting me."

Gregori grunted, then sat down at an adjoining table, facing him. "How'd you get my email address?"

"Kat. She dug around on the black web. Also found your address."

In fact, he'd gotten an earful from Coco on the wisdom of this plan, having known Gregori from her days as a black-hat hacker in Russia. She, too, didn't trust him.

But he'd burned a few bridges when he'd left Russia, so he was out of options.

Gregori gave a nod. "Kat is working for you?"

He recognized digging. "She's a friend. How's Luda?"

"A grandmother. We have a granddaughter who lives in Potsdam." Gregori shot York a look, lifted one side of his mouth. "She would probably want to tell you hello. But I won't tell her that you were here."

York wondered who he was protecting.

"I need to find someone."

Gregori leaned back, took a sip of his beer. Glanced at the band. "They make no sense. Long hair, screaming. This isn't music."

"They're angry. Frustrated. They say what's inside."

Gregori grunted. "Who are you looking for?"

"My fiancée. She went missing in Heidelberg two days ago."

The Russian looked at him. "Another wife?"

York ignored him. "I think a man named Alan Martin took her."

"Martin. The American spy who tried to kill the president."

And of course, Gregori knew—the guy could have even been in cahoots with Petrov and his master plan to derail the American government.

But York didn't care. "Yes. He escaped from prison during transport a little over a week ago, and turned up in Paris, outside a coffee shop where my gir—fiancée just happened to be."

Gregori raised an eyebrow.

"He's onto something—we stopped him from detonating an EMP bomb in Italy. With a man named Ruslan Gustov."

"Gustov."

York let that name sit for a second as Gregori's mouth tightened.

"Word is that you killed him."

"I did."

Another beat.

"And this Ruslan —"

"Is his brother."

Gregori shook his head. "Now, I understand."

Understand? "Are you still in contact with the Bratva?"

"Of course."

"And is Martin still involved with the Petrovs?"

He finished his beer and set it on the table. "Maybe I should just turn you in."

York stilled. Across from him, Roy drew in a breath, ever so slight. But he kept eating.

Gregori laughed. "Ah, *Voron*, you are still so easy."

York didn't move.

"There is a bounty on you, *tovarish*. One million Euros."

At this Roy picked up his glass.

"By whom?" York said quietly.

Gregori grunted. "Ruslan? Petrov? You have enemies, *Voron*."

The list was long—probably started with the boss of the two goons that had worked York over a couple years back in Moscow. They'd wanted to know how much York knew about the attempted assassination of General Boris Stanislov. Why, York wasn't so sure, but he'd bet the thread wound back to Arkady Petrov, standing in the shadow of Putin, his right-hand man.

Truth was, Russia was one successful assassination away from total dictatorship and a return to the cold war. And it didn't have to be the assassination of a Russian leader, either. Kill the American president, and in the chaos, anything could happen.

What was the saying? In the midst of chaos, there is also opportunity. Sun-Tzu, *the Art of War*. Required reading for any world-leader wanna-be.

Gregori finished his drink. Set it on the table. "Some said you were dead. Others said you'd retired, were living in some small town in the woods. But I said the Bird. He is still watching. Hunting."

"I am. I'm hunting my fiancée. Can you ask around?"

"Without trouble?" His gaze followed a pretty girl who carried a tray of fries.

"Even with trouble."

"I start asking and your enemies will know you're alive."

"I don't care what happens. I just want her back."

The Russian's gaze came back to him. "If they find you, they take you. And I can do nothing."

York nodded. Then he reached into his inside pocket and pulled out a burner phone. "There's one number on it."

Gregori pocketed it. Stood up. Sighed. Then he held out his hand. "*Posmatree Zadee.*"

"Regards to Luda."

Gregori. "I'll buy her wine from Moldovia. She'll know."

He left his mug and headed out into the crowd.

"One million Euros. A guy could buy a small yacht with that."

York glanced over at him. Reached for his plate, his appetite stirring, rousing. "What do you need a yacht for? You're a professional tourist."

"A guy can dream."

"I'd rather have land." And, oh, he should probably check in with his realtor, in Shelly, make sure the earnest money went through—

He closed his eyes. He needed to stop thinking like a man who had a life to go back to.

"With that face, you're going to need something stronger than beer," Roy said and shoved his half-full mug over.

"No. What I need is to...I don't know—"

"Breathe. Think. You won't do RJ any good if you keel over. You look a little white."

York nodded. "I could use some shut-eye."

Roy stared at him, almost unseeing. "I'm an idiot."

"What?"

"Ziggy. It's bugging me that she hasn't called me. Not once. I've tried her phone—and I keep getting her voice mail. *Hey you. You know what to do. È una bella giornata. Arrivederci.*"

"I don't speak Italian."

"It's a beautiful day. Not *have* a beautiful day but...a statement. It *is* a beautiful day."

"Roy—"

"It's what she says every morning when she's at her home."

York raised an eyebrow.

"In Tuscany. Where I was going to send you and RJ for a little vacation. Her parents have a vineyard there. Run a little B&B. It's safe and tucked away and...if they got away from Martin, they'd head to Lucca. I'm sure of it."

"Back to Italy."

"She's there, York. I feel it in my bones."

"I hope that's not the bratwurst talking."

He shoved the beer at York. "You just stay alive long enough to get there."

CHAPTER
THREE

If she was going to be lost, hiding and holding out hope that York would find her, this would be the place to hole up.

RJ stood in a borrowed white tee-shirt, barefoot, a sheet wrapped around her and stared out the window as the moon cast over the rolling green hills, the impossibly star-strewn sky, the smell so rich with greenery and life that she could almost forget.

Almost forget that she'd abandoned the man she loved.

Almost forget that she'd been betrayed by her own stupid sense of grand purpose.

Almost forget that someone had nearly been killed protecting her, again.

But surely, they'd be safe, here, at Ziggy's family villa.

Or, *estate*. The sprawling two-century old home sat atop a hill, the drive long and winding past lush chianti grape vines, and low, twisty olive trees until it reached the apex, a hilltop stone home surrounded by spiring cypress trees, and an aura of history.

She'd slept most of the way to Vienna while RJ, of course, stared out the window as the blackness retreated to dawn.

They'd stayed in the train station for their layover, with Ziggy purchasing a tray of *wiener würstels* and mustard from a street vendor and a couple bottles of soda water. RJ picked up some personal toiletries.

They ate and then boarded the morning train to Florence, an all-day trip..

The trek wound them through mountains, with steep hills that careened to deep azure lakes. Quaint villages cast upon the green foothills, dotted with wildflowers, renaissance steeples rising from central churches amongst red-tiled roofs.

As the train drew deeper into Italy, the mountains fell away, giving over to an undulating landscape of rows and rows of grapevines that climbed up hillsides upon which perched grand clay-tiled roofed homes with arched windows and sprawling terraces.

Hana sat quiet, her eyes wide as the Tuscan countryside unfolded, the last rays of the day gilding the rolling hills. As far as RJ could see, tiny villages squatted on the hilltops, many of them cordoned by tall stone walls, iron gates and watchtowers.

"Those were tiny empires, built in medieval times, were often controlled by the local priests or bishops. A massive catholic church usually sits in the center square, and many have monasteries. A few have castles, too." Ziggy sat in the front seat, turned around like a tour guide.

RJ's spirits began to lift, despite the thunderstorm that came up, spitting upon the train as they finally rolled into Florence.

At least they'd be safe. And she had to believe that somehow, York would find her.

The sky had cleared by the time their taxi arrived, the sun

burning away the clouds, turning the world a watery orange. She got her only good glimpse of the Mattucci estate in the final hour of sunlight, turning the home a deep umber as they drove into the courtyard.

The house, three stone-built stories under a terracotta thatched roof, with green shutters and thick wrought-iron had clearly been built in stages, with the main house added after the smaller villa, set off to the side, with arched windows and a large terrace.

Thick clematis vines clung to the walls of both houses, lush with delicate purple flowers, and pink begonias spilled out of massive terracotta pots planted by the rounded wooden double door to the main house.

The driver let them off, and RJ stood for a bit in the cobblestone drive of the home, caught in the splendor. "This is breathtaking."

Hana found a kitty, and chased it across the drive, toward the back of the house.

"You live in a postcard." She glanced at Ziggy, who was getting out, retrieving her backpack and tipping the driver with euros.

She hiked one side of the pack over her shoulder. Took in the view, then, "No. I live in a two-room flat in a city with a view of the building next door. But my parents live on 30,000 acres of ancient chianti vineyard, complete with wine grottos for our casks, a pressing house, a fermenting room and a terrazzo for tastings."

RJ gave her a look. "Tastings?"

"It's a working winery. And an inn, which is why I had to make sure they had room for us. But right now, they only have one guest coming, so I booked us a couple rooms."

"I thought it was a safe house." She'd envisioned a tiny,

windowless house with bodyguards, dogs and maybe a perimeter fence.

"Look around. Do you feel safe?" Ziggy smiled, one of the first she'd seen. The woman had a beauty deep in her bones she probably didn't even realize.

RJ met her smile. "I feel hidden in a storybook."

"Perfect. I promise, you'll be safe here." Ziggy headed off after Hana, and RJ followed her. They passed under an arbor, following a cobblestone path toward the back of the house.

"My great-great grandfather Massimo built the main house, and the cottage house was converted into the summer kitchen, around the turn of the century. He was the true vintner in the family. He took our chianti grapes and crafted wine that started winning awards.

"We sell wine all over the world, but it's all from one core root that my great-great-great-*great* grandfather brought from an estate in eastern Italy. He worked as an assistant groundskeeper of the Barone estate, and during Italy's first War of Independence, in 1849, the estate was captured and burned. Alfonzo escaped with a graft of the vine root. He gave it to his wife, Gemma, for safekeeping while he was conscripted into the military. Alfonzo served under the Grand Duchy of Tuscany and was discharged with honors. The Duchy gave him this plot of land as a reward. He planted his first vineyard from the graft and...the rest is history."

"The rest is heaven," RJ said as they stopped in the back courtyard.

A cool, inviting blue pool spanned the yard, tall cypress trees cordoning it and beyond it, the striking view of the pastoral landscape turned the world at once immense and calm.

It reminded her of her family's home in Montana. Maybe

not as much history, but still, a part of the land, the landscape of time. A legacy upon the earth.

It stirred something deep inside her that she couldn't name.

"Oh!"

The cry came from an older woman as she dodged Hana and the kitty. Late sixties, perhaps, with silvery hair piled behind her head. Lean, and dressed in a pair of jeans, a floral blouse, she carried a watering pitcher, wore a pair of worn, dirty fabric gardening gloves, and matching tennis shoes.

"Tssk. Tssk," Hana said, and the sound nudged something inside RJ. A memory. She couldn't wrap her fingers around it.

"Mamma Tessa," Ziggy said and approached the woman, speaking in Italian.

Hana chased the kitty under the shade of a portico and scooped it up around the belly. Nuzzled her face into the gray fur.

For a second RJ was a seven-year-old girl chasing cats on her family's ranch, running into the cool of the barn.

"This is RJ," Ziggy said, bringing the woman over.

"RJ, this is my Mamma, Tessa."

The woman had removed her gloves and now pulled RJ close and kissed her on each cheek. "Benvenuto." She had Ziggy's aquiline nose, high cheekbones, her full lips, but green eyes. "Are you hungry?"

And that's how RJ found herself, an hour later, sitting at the long, rough-hewn table with Tessa and Ziggy's father, Santini, under the lights of the portico eating Tuscan fish stew, with tomatoes, clams, anchovies, halibut, shrimp and a host of fresh herbs she'd watched Tessa cut from pots. A half-cut loaf of crusty Italian bread and fresh cheese sat on a board in the middle of the table.

Santini might have been the most handsome seventy-two-year-old Italian RJ had ever met—full salt and pepper hair, broad shoulders, deeply tanned, white smile, deep-blue eyes. He wore linen pants, a gauzy open shirt, and canvas shoes. And when he laughed his gaze always returned to Tessa, as if everything hinged on her smile.

Reminded her a little of her own parents, once upon a time, before her father's heart attack. Maybe even a little of her mother and her new husband, Hardwin.

Maybe that's how marriage was supposed to be—depending on each other for a smile, as if it might be part of your breath, your soul.

She didn't deserve for York to chase after her, maybe. No, probably.

Tessa had uncorked a magnum of their table chianti that had only made RJ wish she had a more developed palate, and served it with cheese for dessert.

By the time they finished eating, the moon had risen, silvering the rolling hills, the stars cascading over the far mountains. Hana had fallen asleep on the bench beside RJ, the kitty in her embrace.

"Is she your daughter?" Tessa sat at the end of the table in a worn wooden chair, padded, holding her wine, still only half-drunk, a piece of gouda in her hand.

"No. It's a long story. I'm watching her," RJ said. She hadn't exactly known what to do with Hana after they'd escaped from the hospital. "She went through a trauma and doesn't speak, so..."

"She speaks," Tessa said. She nodded toward the kitty. "They had a long chat."

"It takes time for some people to trust." She looked at Ziggy. "Especially after they've been hurt. But children bounce back."

Ziggy looked at her, smiled. "If they are loved."

Tessa smiled, and a sweetness fell over the table.

"Did Ziggy tell you the history around our villa?" Santini asked.

"A little. She told me about Alfonzo and Gemma, Massimo and also about Sigfrid. Said he was an American GI."

Santini looked at Ziggy. Raised an eyebrow. "Really." He took a sip of wine. "She does like that story."

A heaviness fell into the air.

Ziggy, strangely, just stared away.

"It's a sad story," Tessa said. "But yes, one we shouldn't ignore." She looked pointedly at Santini. "It's worth telling."

He glanced at her, then Ziggy. "I suppose." He picked up his wine. "Tessa's mother, Angelica hid him on those grottos right over there." He pointed toward a hill beyond the cottage. "If you want to visit tomorrow, I can ask Lucio to give you a tour."

"Oh, I don't need a tour."

"You must have a tour," Tessa said. "All our guests get a tour of the grounds, the grotto."

Guests? That's right—Ziggy had said it was an inn. "You have a lot of guests?"

"We rent out rooms occasionally. For people who want to experience a working vineyard. I teach cooking classes, and Santini sells the wine."

"*Serves* the wine. The *vino* sells herself." He winked.

Tessa raised her glass, her gaze finding his. Smiled, and the heaviness lifted. Then Tessa turned to RJ. "We're glad you're here. Stay as long as you'd like."

They'd have to kick her out.

Tessa helped RJ lead a sleepy Hana to a room on the third floor, small, single bed with a yellow coverlet. They tucked in the kitty next to her.

"Don't worry about her," Tessa said. "She'll talk when she's ready."

Then Tessa showed her to the room next door. The wooden floors creaked as she entered. The window overlooked the pool area, the furniture had to be antique, but freshly polished, but a crisp white duvet covered the double bed, and fresh yellow roses filled a vase on the bedside table.

"Sleep well," Tessa said as she let herself out.

Not a chance. RJ didn't know if it was the buzz of the past couple days, but as she climbed into the double bed, under crisp white sheets, she stared at the wooden beams of the ceiling, the glass chandelier catching the moonlight and knew she should be on her honeymoon.

She finally got up, wrapped the sheet around her. And now stood at the window.

Find me, York.

A knock on the door turned her. "Come in."

The door eased open, and Ziggy came in, wearing a pair of track pants and a tee-shirt, her hair down. "I heard the floor creak and thought you might be up."

"I'm exhausted, but my brain won't shut off."

Ziggy was carrying a book. "I get that." She held out the book. Worn blue cover, the spine loose. "It's a memoir, written by my Nonna Angelica. Published in Italian in the 1980s, then translated into English in the early nineties. It's the story of Fred and the Italian resistance and...I thought you might enjoy it. It's actually been optioned for a movie, so we'll see. But that was years ago, so, probably nothing will come of it. Still. Like Mamma Tessa said, it's worth telling."

RJ took the book. Opened it. A signature was scrawled in black ink on the front page. *To Sigfrid, love Nonna.* "This is your copy?"

"One of the few that remain. It was a small printing." Ziggy came to stand by the window. "I love it here at night. The wind in the trees, the smell of the vines. It was a beautiful place to grow up, especially after my parents died."

RJ frowned. "What?"

Ziggy turned to her. "Tessa and Santini are my aunt and uncle. My parents were killed in a car accident when I was four. Mamma Tessa and Papà Santini adopted me. Tessa was my father's half-sister."

No wonder Ziggy didn't remotely resemble her father.

"Papà Santini doesn't like talking about my parents."

"Why not?"

"Santini dated my mother before Sigfrid married her."

Oh. But his comment, and the silence after it, felt like more than just an old jealousy. And the conversation had been about her grandfather, not her father. Then again, RJ was tired, and it was possible her instincts weren't firing right. "Your father was named Sigfrid too?"

"After Fred. Family name, remember?"

"Right."

"It's a taboo subject for Papà. Apparently, he wanted to marry Carlita, my mother, but Sigfrid had been abroad, in America, and when he returned, he swept Carlita off her feet. Married her out from under Santini. She was twenty-four. Sigfrid was thirty." She turned back to the window. "It took them seventeen years before they had me."

"Wow."

"Yes. A couple miscarriages at the beginning, and then nothing for years. My mother had me at forty-one. Meanwhile, Santini had married Momma Tessa, and by that time, I had cousins who were ten and twelve years older than me. Felix, who lives in Rome, and Bella, in New York, who is a doctor."

"No one lives at the winery?"

Ziggy headed toward the door. "It's a hard business. And it has to be in the blood, I think."

"You don't want it?"

"I have a different life." Ziggy reached for the door. Paused. "For now." Then she turned back to RJ. "By the way, I was able to charge my phone and download my voice mails. Roy left a message. He and York are on the way." She smiled. "I told you everything would be okay." She smiled and closed the door.

But RJ stood at the window, the book clasped to her.

She'd heard that before.

"Gotta love Italy."

York barely heard Roy, who sat beside him in a very cramped Fiat 500, his window down, the wind in his hair as it swept off the Mediterranean Sea to the west.

"Yeah," York said softly.

Really, he was just being paranoid.

No one was following him. No one had sat in the threadbare lobby of his hotel room last night, waiting until morning when he and Roy left for Rome. No one had followed them to the Berlin Brandenburg Airport, sat across from him in the terminal during the two-hour flight delay, then boarded the plane and sat three rows behind him.

And no one was on their tail three cars back on their drive up the coast of Italy on a slick black Ducati Streetfighter V4 motorcycle.

A real beauty if you asked him.

And certainly, driving it *wasn't* the thirty-something man with short brown hair, scraggly brown beard, wide face, wearing a pair of faded black jeans and a black jean jacket he'd seen at the hotel. At the airport and even on the plane. York might not have noticed him at all except for the tattoos on his fingers—Nazi symbols that didn't match his exterior, visible as he sat in the dismal breakfast area of their cheap hotel, watching the flat screen, nursing a coffee and a stale danish.

York couldn't put a finger on what it was about him—maybe he looked familiar. Call it a feeling, but York had glanced at him on their way out the door and found the man's gaze on him something in the man's eyes had needled him.

It was just Gregori's words sticking in his head, *There is a bounty on you, tovarish. One million Euros.*

Which, he supposed, might make anyone paranoid, but it wasn't the first time someone had hunted him.

He was getting soft.

"You all right?" Roy sat in the driver's seat of their rental car. York's knees were nearly in his lap, and Roy looked like he might be driving a go-cart, his knees up around the steering wheel, even as he shifted into gear. At least they were out of the snarl of traffic after landing at Leonardo Da Vinci Airport over two hours ago, standing in a line for over an hour in the rental area, and grabbing the last compact available.

"Yeah," York said, and glanced in the rear-view mirror. Yep, only now two cars back, leaning over the road bike, helmeted and geared up in leather. "Feeling a ghost."

"Gregori's words getting to you?"

"I'm just tired." He turned back around. He'd slept an hour, maybe more last night, staring at the stains in the ceiling, Roy snoring from the other queen bed. What he'd really wanted was answers, but nothing came to him, so by morning he'd showered, his wound still covered in a sort of plastic sheath they'd given him at the hospital, shaved, put on fresh jeans, re-tucked RJ's engagement ring into his front pocket, donned a tee-shirt and felt relatively awake when he'd placed a call to his boss, Logan Thorne, in D.C.

The director of the Caleb Group, the private security think

tank and concessional *get it done* group put together by President Isaac White was probably out running at the five-a.m. hour because he didn't pick up.

Usually, the man had the phone glued to him.

York left a terse message, something about calling him back, then drank about a half-gallon of coffee and headed to the airport with Roy.

"How long until we get there?"

"Four hours, plus," Roy said.

Despite York's hurry to see RJ, he couldn't ignore the beauty of the shoreline. The drive brought them along the cliff that dropped some fifty to a hundred feet to the glorious Mediterranean Sea, so blue under the fading sunlight it seemed to stretch on forever. Calm, a few sailboats dotting the water, the sun low and reaching out an orange finger to touch the water.

Breathe. "It is nice." He glanced out of the mirror. Didn't see the cyclist, but a truck had turned in between him and the potential tail.

Yep, paranoid.

He closed his eyes. "How do you know this place?"

"The Mattucci estate? It's in Ziggy's family."

"How do you know Ziggy?"

"Her partner and I did some job together. After he died, Ziggy filled in. She's smart. Tough. Her family were resistance fighters in World War Two, working against Mussolini, and then Hitler. Helped hide and transport Jews to safety, and then, later, American and British fliers who got caught behind enemy lines." He downshifted and pulled out, passed a slow moving, late model Lancia hatchback, putting the gas all the way to the floor.

"Should I get out and push?"

"I miss my Maserati." He slipped back into his lane.

"You have a Maserati?" York shook his head. "I need to ask for a raise."

Roy smiled.

"So, is there something between you and Ziggy?"

Roy glanced in the rear-view mirror. "He's still there."

"Who?" York hazarded a look. Shoot. The cyclist had also pulled out, passing the truck.

"If he's trying not to be noticed, he's doing a poor job," Roy said. "I spotted him at the hotel, and then at the Berlin airport."

"And the plane."

"Hard to miss, with those tats."

"He has a cleft palate."

"Maybe it's not him."

Roy nodded. He down shifted as they climbed a hill, the road dropping off to their left to the sea, foamy as it crested against the cliff side below.

"What if she's not there."

"She will be. Ziggy texted last night, one word. Ciao. They're there, York."

He looked out the window, his hands on his jeans

Overhead, the sky was darkening, the clouds gray and heavy, maybe evidence of the storm that had delayed their flight, now gathering in southwestern Tuscany.

"We're coming up to a town—Civitavecchia. Want to grab some grub?"

"I want to be there already," York said. He glanced at the cyclist. He hadn't advanced on them. "But yes, I'm starved."

"There's an Autogrill ahead." Roy nodded towards a building on the side of the road, the words, providentially, *Autogrill,* on a sign above the building.

They pulled in, and York got out, watching for the cyclist.

He motored by without a pause, and York watched him disappear down the highway.

The nearby sea reefed a coolness into the air, the hills on the eastern side green and forested.

They walked into the massive building, more of a convenience store with pumps, but with a deli and food preparation station. Families sat at tables eating panini sandwiches from the deli case, the parents drinking coffee. The air smelled of fresh bread, He stood for a long time in front of the deli case, choosing between two sandwiches—a mozzarella with *prosciutto di parma*, and a *camogli*, made with focaccia, ham and *emmental* cheese.

He finally chose the *camogli*, took it over to the table where Roy was downing something that looked like a sub, only with burrata cheese, bologna and garnished with pistachio, on focaccia.

"This is some serious fast food."

"I love Italy," Roy said. "You missed out working the Eastern bloc countries all those years."

York slid into the booth and spread out his sandwich. A woman brought over a cup of espresso in a real mug. "Spoken like a man who's never eaten a fresh pork *Cheboriki* dripping with grease from an old babushka selling them from a tin pot."

Roy grinned. "Back when spies were spies."

"And real men didn't care if they had salad with their bread. I once lived for a week on a trip into the Siberian bush with a slab of white, smoked *sala* and vodka."

"Hunting."

"Mmmhmm." York bit into the sandwich. "Okay, this is good."

Roy grinned and looked out the window. "You should get RJ and go home."

York took a sip of the coffee. "Now you're thinking about Gregori's words."

He met York's gaze. "Let me and Ziggy handle it. Whatever this is. Take RJ and go back to your life."

"What if she doesn't want to? I'm starting to think RJ's definition of love and mine are vastly different."

"I had to pry her away from your bedside, York. This is my fault." He met York's eyes with a grim face. "I'm sorry."

He took another bite, half done. Wiped his mouth. "Listen, when I was back in Shelly, with no memory, I got a good look at what life looked like without regret. Right then, God set me free—I had no idea what from, until I got my memory back but by then I realized that I could still be free. If I believe that God has a plan for my life, then there are no mistakes, no regrets, just moments that God carries me. Moments when I'm forced to trust him."

Roy had finished his sandwich. "You sound like Hamilton Jones, my old SEAL team leader."

"I've met Ham. I'll take that as a compliment."

"He's a good man. Used to tell us that when we're stuck, and we can't see a way out, even while we're trying to figure a way out, God has already gone before us. We just have to remember our training and take one step at a time."

He cleaned his face, then balled up the napkin. "What's your next step, York?"

He considered Roy. The man had been tortured by the Taliban, escaped and then been forced into service for the CIA. Still, he'd made a sort of peace with his life, it seemed. As if he knew who he was, was content with where he woke up every morning.

"I know I love RJ."

Roy nodded. "And she loves you, I know it. But you do need

to figure out if that means you two belong together." His mouth made a grim line. "I'm hitting the head. See you in five."

York finished his sandwich, his coffee.

By the time he finished his coffee, Roy had moved the car to a pump. "Just thought we should fill up."

York scanned the parking lot. No motorcycle, just a couple big tankers and a few family sedans.

The sun had sunk behind the city as they drove through it then away from the shore. Shadows cast over the road as they climbed into the hills, past farmland. Night fell, the land dotted with lights from far away houses, the moon rising, an orange ball to the east.

Roy's phone buzzed in the panel between the seats and York picked it up. "Logan."

"I got your message. What's up?"

York filled him in on the hunt for RJ, and his meeting with Gregori. "He said there's a bounty on me. I'd like to know who put it out there."

"Sure. I'll get Coco on it. Where are you guys right now?"

"Italy. Headed up to a friend's villa in Tuscany."

"It's ninety degrees and smoggy here. I should be on a plane."

"You and me both."

"Eat some pasta for me."

York grinned and hung up.

Maybe he should just calm down. Of course he and RJ belonged together. He was just tired, strung out, still hurting, maybe a little paranoid—

"Lights, behind us York."

He glanced in the mirror. Three lights, a large one in the middle, two on the side. "A motorcycle."

"Think it's our friend?"

Roy said nothing as the lights suddenly moved up on them. Closer.

"Put it down."

"It's already on the floor," Roy said, glanced in the rear-view mirror.

Now York *really* wanted Roy's Maserati.

The motorcycle edged up, then sat on their bumper.

"Brakes?"

"What if it's not...anyone. I'll kill him," Roy said.

Then the cyclist pulled out. Ahead, the road was clear, so he could be passing—

The window behind Roy shattered. York ducked, and Roy swerved, hitting the ditch, slamming his brakes. The cyclist sped by.

"What was that?"

Roy flicked on the interior light as York turned. A rock the size of a softball lay on the seat, surrounded by glass. "Why would —"

"He's coming back." Roy flicked off the lights even as York turned around.

Then Roy gunned it aiming for the motorcycle. "He's someone."

York braced his arm on the dash.

The motorcycle turned off his lights. Still, with their head-lights, they could make him out.

Shots, two, pinged off the car even as he sped by them.

Their headlights pinged out. Roy bit back a word and hit the brakes.

"What is he playing at?" York said.

He turned. In the silver of the moonlight, he made out the bike turning, heading back. "This isn't good. Lights, Roy."

Just as the motorcycle sped by, something pinged into the back seat.

York spotted it and his heart just—stopped. Then, "Grenade!" He reached for the door and threw himself out.

Rolled.

The car exploded. A plume of fire mushroomed into the night. York covered his head with his hands, kept rolling.

Fell into a ditch.

He scrambled to his knees. "Roy!"

Up the road, the motorcycle had turned, headed back.

York found his footing, scrabbled up the embankment to the burning car. "Roy!"

He didn't see a body burning to death, but the blaze roared.

Shots. They pinged off the car and York ducked back into the ditch.

But the fire illuminated his attacker, and as the motorcycle neared, his hands landed on a good-sized rock, larger than the one that had broken the fiat's window.

He measured the distance and then, as the man came into the light, he fired at the wheel.

The rider must have seen it because he jerked the bike to avoid the projectile.

His attempt turned the front wheel just enough—the rock struck the side of the front tire, the bike wavered, skidded and went down. It spun out on the pavement, headed toward the opposite ditch. The man spilled off.

Bullseye.

York took off, headed toward the attacker and landed on him just as he pushed himself off the pavement. Helmeted, the man seemed barely shaken by his road rash, and York kicked him in the gut, hoping to send him back to the ground.

It worked, but the man rolled, found his knees and popped up, still helmeted.

But unarmed.

York spotted a pistol—looked like a .22 magnum, semi—

under the firelight, some ten feet away. Probably held ten rounds, plus, and he'd pulled off three, maybe five.

If the magazine had been full, he had six bullets left.

York leaped for the gun.

The man leaped on him, and he woofed to the ground, some two hundred pounds on him. Worse the man had uncanny aim—he kneed York in the back.

York howled—didn't care—but rolled and sent a fist into the man's groin.

Turnabout.

His attacker fell back, and York reached for the gun.

Gone.

He turned back. His attacker was fighting to get to his feet, then he fell back, the gun out.

Fired.

Missed, although York felt the heat of it tan his cheek.

He rolled as the man sent off another shot, then again, all the way to the other side of the road.

Where he found Roy, who grabbed him down.

"Where have you been?"

"Reconnaissance."

In the firelight, he spotted a red rash down Roy's face, blood in his eyes, his arm at a strange angle.

"Now what?"

"Here," Roy said and slapped something into York's hand.

A grenade. "Where —"

"While you two were wrestling, I unpacked his bike. He's got a small armory in there. But I have bad aim." He was looking past York, and now pointed.

York turned. The man had found his feet, had started for them.

York pulled the pin and tossed the grenade.

Roy grabbed him and they rolled down into the well of the ditch.

The grenade detonated and for a long moment he didn't move.

Then, he popped up.

Roy was ahead of him, scrabbling up the embankment. He shot a look at the attacker. "Oh. Well, the helmet worked."

York winced.

Pieces—although his body was still on his head. He got up and walked over to the body, then lifted the visor.

"I wasn't being paranoid." He turned away.

Roy came up, looking like the terminator, bloody, in pieces, grim and angry. "Gregori?"

York gave another look at the man. "Maybe."

"My cell phone was in the car," Roy said.

"The bike is wrecked." York had walked over to examine the machine, hoping.

Too bad. It was a nice bike.

"We should grab some of those munitions," Roy said.

York looked at him. "And be arrested as terrorists? Look at you. We need to find a hospital."

Roy had walked over to the ditch, staring at the burning Fiat.

York joined him. "You're not getting your deposit back."

"At least I wasn't driving the Maserati."

Roy looked at him and York met it with a shake of his head, a wry grin.

Then he turned away from Roy, the burning car, the moonlight, and stared at the road ahead, a light in the distance. "Gotta love Italy."

Then he put Roy's good arm over his shoulder, and they headed up the road.

CHAPTER FOUR

Chapter 7/Portami a casa: un ricordo della resistenza italiana

I'd left him in the grotto, behind a wall of wine casks, on a pallet. He had barely roused when Arturo and I retrieved him from the field, and even when I removed his shirt and pulled the bullet out of the terrible wound in his back. When he didn't die the first night, breaking out in a fever instead, I wanted to fetch the doctor, but Arturo forbid it.

He doesn't want the stranger here. Doesn't want me to feed him, tend him.

Arturo knows the dangers. He is the one who visits the monastery in the valley, retrieves the news from the other hilltop cities.

The other couriers. So, of course he is afraid—we all are.

Not that Arturo should tell me what to do, his employer, how to run our estate, but in truth I lean on him so much now that Papa is gone.

And Mamma is resigned to despair.

And perhaps he is right. With the Nazis now taking harbor in Lucca, berthing at local residences, it is only a matter of time before they will decide that the estate of Mattucci is their next headquarters, the house big enough to house a squad of jackboots, the summer kitchen a place of meeting.

And with Tory gone most nights, it would only bring upon us more questions.

Danger.

Thus, I feared to find a corpse when I returned the next morning with a bowl of hot polenta, fresh grape juice and crusty bread.

Instead, our traveler is gone.

I stand in the cool breath of the grotto, the dark walls casting shadow upon the wooden casks of our last batch of Chianti before Papa's execution, my heart a fist in my chest.

He has gone. Escaped back into the night from whence he appeared, and perhaps I should agree that we are the better for it.

But my chest is empty, and I don't know why.

More than anything, I long for the peace that has been stolen from me. I long for life, and freedom.

I long for hope.

Perhaps I thought this stranger would bring it.

Behind is the pallet on the floor, a blanket, a sheet, grimy with blood and the debris of rough living. And, with it, a deep-seated hope that we might be freed from the danger hidden beyond, in the darkest corner of the grotto.

"Signora?"

The voice is deep, and vibrates inside me, perhaps to my soul, so unexpected, so deeply longed for that the realization rattles me.

What? Do I believe this man is my savior?

I turn, and am as equally nonplussed to find him shirtless, his skin glistening with water, as if he has bathed in the pond behind the estate.

He might be the most beautiful man I've ever seen. Dark curly hair, almost woolen on his head. Bright golden-brown eyes. And with a form that betrays hard work, sculpted arms, fine pectoral muscles, a lean, washboard stomach. Clad in his camo pants, he has narrow hips, lean legs and stands over six feet, although that might be in my mind, for his stature suddenly envelopes me.

I am a dreamer, and this man has dropped into my world, wounded, yes but a lifeline.

Perhaps the one I have prayed for.

I am also terribly aware of my own attire—a cotton dress dusted in flour, my hair tied up in a faded floral, albeit clean, scarf, and I'm thinner than I would like. My feet, in sandals, are dirty from the dust from the fields. "Signore."

"Sigfrid." He takes a step toward me. He is holding his shirt, and it is wet, so he must have washed it. Now he grips it in one hand and holds out the other. "But my friends call me Fred."

His words are English, of course, but my father, who dealt with international buyers, taught both Tory and me some German, English and even French.

I know enough to take his hand. "How are you?"

"Better, thank you." He seems embarrassed now, but smiles. "I think you saved my life."

Probably, yes. "I took the bullet out." It hadn't lodged deep, but barely missed his spine, so perhaps providence also saved him. "And brought you to our estate. You were in poor state."

"Thank you. It took great courage."

Not courage at all. I feared, if he were found by anyone else, it would rouse suspicion.

Bring the Germans to our door.

And then they might find Tory and discover his recent activities. I will do anything to protect my brother.

But I am now wondering if, in my fear, God has provided an answer.

Fred looks around the grotto. I wonder if he sees what I see—our entire future, our cash crop in barrels, waiting, aging, but also hidden from those who would steal it. The grotto extends further into the hill, of course, and I hope he doesn't look too far, wander past the bend.

The grotto is quiet, save for our voices, swallowed by the sandstone, and for that, I am thankful.

"Where am I?"

"Estate Mattucci. Outside Lucca. You were in our fields."

He nods.

A pause as his gaze searches mine, a question in his expression.

"You are safe here."

His chest rises and falls. Then, he nods.

It is then I realize I'm holding the porridge. I set the wooden tray on a nearby cask. "You must stay in the grotto. There are German patrols."

I don't mention the request. Not yet. Not until he is ready to travel.

"Thank you." He picked up the bowl of polenta, a piece of the crusty bread. "And yes, I will. I'm sorry."

I want to know more. Where is he from? How did he arrive here?

"Let me see your wound." My voice is my protector, it betrays nothing of my thoughts, my fears.

He draws in a breath, but nods and turns, showing me my handiwork in his back. It is inflamed, of course, but his body seems to be fighting it. "I will make you a poultice. It should take down the swelling."

"Are you a doctor?" He dips the bread into the polenta.

"No. But my mother is an herbalist—or she was. And I've doctored my brother's wounds."

With the bite of bread, he makes a sound deep in his chest, almost a growl, except in pleasure. He swallows. "Heaven."

Then he smiles, full on, something bright and beautiful.

It is as if the world has tilted beneath my feet, the sunrise taking me into its embrace. Hot, blinding, healing, overwhelming.

I can feel it in my bones, this instant rush of desire and it terrifies me.

No. I am simply lonely. Tired. Afraid. Needy. And this stranger, who has risen almost miraculously from his sick bed is not a redeemer, but a danger.

I must remember that, despite my hope.

"Your wound is healing." I also check the place on his forehead where it looks like he fell. A bruise, a hint of swelling. My fingers touch his skin, and he draws in a breath.

"Does it hurt?"

He shakes his head and I draw my hand away, my heart in my throat.

"What is your name?" His voice is soft.

"Angelica," I whisper, my voice betraying me.

"Angel." His golden-eye gaze holds mine.

I am rooted, although inside, I want to flee.

"Signora?"

The young voice shatters the moment and I turn, the taste of horror in my throat to see young Bertie in the entrance of the cave. Five years old, barefoot, dressed in work clothes, he must have come with his father to dress the vines. His blue eyes are wide, curious.

"Bertie!" I head toward him, wanting to shush him, to send him back to Arturo where his father can dissuade him from asking about the man in the shadows. But I don't want Arturo to know. So, I crouch in front of him. "Would you like breakfast. I've made you porridge in the kitchen."

Those blue eyes alight, he nods, then turns and scampers off.

I turn, afraid of what he's seen.

Fred is gone, vanished into the darkness of the grotto.

Returning to the cask, I retrieve the tray of empty porridge. The bread is gone, as is the flask of juice.

But from the darkness I feel his eyes on me, watching. Pulling me into something I can't voice.

So, I run. Because he is not a savior.

He will cost us everything.

RJ woke with her hand on the book, having fallen asleep, her dreams playing out the scene between Fred and Angel.

She knew exactly how it felt to have someone walk into your life, to shake your world, to cling to him like a savior.

Except York hadn't cost her everything. Truth was, she'd been the force of destruction in his life, bringing him over to America where his past could hunt him down.

And now, he had vanished again.

Shoot.

How did this get so far out of control?

She pushed out of bed, and stood at the window, her gaze going to the hillside grotto. A giant wooden door was open to the darkness inside, and she could too easily imagine Angel standing in the entrance, holding breakfast.

A thought to which her stomach responded with a growl.

Ziggy had left her a change of clothes - a pair of linen pants, a pink tee-shirt and along with the toiletries she'd picked up at the Vienna train station, RJ managed to put a dent in her self-respect in the blue tiled bathroom, braiding her dark hair as she came out of the bedroom.

The smell of eggs in butter, some sort of fresh bread baking and roasted meat drew her downstairs to the kitchen.

She'd stepped back in time, maybe a half-century to a grand eat-in kitchen under a brick archway between the kitchen and long dining table.

In the kitchen area, a patterned orange and blue tile spanned the wall, with white-washed cupboards that stretched on either side of a massive plaster hood. Below it, pots sat on a six-burner range. And next to that, a massive wood-fed, white-washed brick oven spoke of simpler days. A set of stainless-steel double ovens banked the other end of the cabinets. A spray of yellow roses sat in a blue and white tile pot on the black granite countertop and polished terracotta tile cooled her bare feet.

The place should be in a picture book of villas to love in Italy.

Tessa stood at a long roughhewn worktable that looked about a century old, sturdy, with stories etched in its worn top. She kneaded dough in a bowl, an apron around her middle, her hair held back, humming.

Hana sat across from her on a wooden chair, eating a bowl of what looked like corn porridge, raspberries and honey stirred in. A giant piece of bread lay on a plate, smothered in honey. She held a crayon, and was drawing a picture with one hand, her hand gripping the bread with the other. It looked like a kitty—round face, pointed ears, whiskers.

Tessa looked up. "*Buongiorno!*" She picked up a towel and wiped her floured hands. "Ziggy has left already. She told me she'd be back in a few hours."

"Where'd she go?"

"I don't know. She never really tells me. I know she works as a tourist guide, but sometimes her work confuses me."

RJ said nothing, came over and slid onto a chair beside Hana, who looked up at her. Someone had freshly braided her hair, given her a new dress and she glanced up at Tessa who smiled, winked.

"I have fresh polenta with raspberries, if you'd like some." Tessa left the dough to grab an earthenware bowl from the shelf. She ladled polenta from a pot into it, dropped some fresh butter in the middle and added raspberries and some fresh cream. Then she walked over to the table and set it in front of RJ. "*Buon appetito.*"

A board with bread and a knife lay in the center of the table, a bowl with what looked like fresh honey, including the honeycomb on the board next to it. RJ cut herself a piece of bread, and then, thinking of the story, she dipped it into the polenta like Fred.

"Now you eat like an Italian." Tessa returned to her kneading.

"I was reading the memoir. What does, *Portami a casa* mean?"

"Bring me home. I suppose Ziggy gave you her English copy?"

"Yes. It's very...compelling."

Tessa looked up. "Wait until you get to the love scene."

"There's a love scene?"

"How do you think Ziggy got here? She is Sigfrid's direct descendant."

"And you're not?"

Tessa laughed, even as she took out a long, thin rolling pin. "No. Sigfrid wasn't my father. His son was my half-brother. He was ten years older than me. She'd floured the table, and now cut the dough into pieces. "My father was a man named Rafael Gabrielli. He married my mother after the war. Good man. He loved Sig, despite, well, despite Sig not being his."

"What happened to the original Sigfrid."

Tess looked up. "Oh, I can't give away the ending." She winked, then began to flatten the dough onto the table with the rolling pin.

"So, you're not a Mattucci."

"It's my maiden name, but technically, no, Santini's last name is Fonda. But Ziggy—she bears the family name. The family legacy."

She watched Tessa roll out the dough, fold it, then roll it out again, thinner. "What are you making?"

"Spaghetti."

"I thought that was bread."

"No, see, it's not as elastic as bread. And it's more orange. That's the eggs." She held up a thicker piece, then put it back on the board and folded it over onto itself. "The key is to keep rolling it out until it becomes paper thin. Then, you cut it and let it dry, just a little. Or, put it fresh in the pot."

She gestured to a drying rack, on the counter.

Oh, to cook like Tessa.

The thought stirred inside her. Wait—what? The last thing RJ had ever wanted to be was domestic. Her idea of making pasta involved boiling water and a blue box of Kraft.

It was possible Tessa could also read minds because she looked at RJ, then at Hana. "Would you like to try?"

"Yes."

"Finish your polenta. You and Hana can roll out the next ones."

RJ picked up a spoon, then turned to Hana. The little girl had set down her bread on the table, was holding her paper and coloring the kitty orange. "I like your kitty."

Hana looked at her.

"You know—*meow, meow*." She made the sound.

And just like that Hana smiled, her blue eyes brightening, and she laughed.

The sound if it washed through RJ like a fragrance and she just stared at the girl. Then, Hana pointed to her picture. "Tssk, Tssk."

And again, the noise moved inside RJ.

Wait—

It was the same sound Coco, her Russian foster sister had

made when she moved to the ranch, running after their fluffy kitties.

"Hana, *tee gavorish po-russki?*"

Hana stilled, then nodded. "*Da.*"

Yes.

She looked at Tessa, back to Hana. "She's Russian."

Tessa looked at the little girl. "Really. Where did you find her?"

"In a German cancer ward."

"She doesn't look like she has cancer."

RJ turned to Hana. "*Tee ne bolni?*"

Hana frowned, shook her head.

RJ also frowned. "*Pocheymo tee okazalus v bolnitza?*"

Hana shrugged.

"She has no idea why she was in the hospital."

Tessa's eyes narrowed. "Who brought her there?"

RJ translated the question.

Hana turned back to her paper. Answered her softly. *I don't know. People came to the orphanage and took me.*

A chill brushed through RJ. "I think she was kidnapped. Or maybe sold."

"The poor thing," Tessa said. She came around the table, crouched next to Hana, who looked up and then held up the picture. Tessa nodded, said something in Italian.

"Okay, time to cook," Tessa said and stood up. She took a bread towel of a folded stack in a nearby basket and held it up, corner to corner.

Hana hopped off the bench and Tessa tied it around her waist.

"Want one?" Tessa asked.

"Why not." RJ took the towel and tied it around her waist.

Tessa gave her a piece of pasta dough, another to Hana,

floured Hana's part of the table and instructed RJ to do the same. Then she handed both of them rolling pins. Not the heavy kind RJ might find at her mother's house, but thinner, longer.

"Press down hard," Tessa said, standing behind Hana, holding her hands as they pressed down together.

RJ had thought Hana shy. Instead, she'd simply been silenced by the language barrier. Now, she giggled as Tessa helped her roll out the pasta.

Not as easy as it looked, really. Tessa and Hana had their pasta rolled long before RJ was handed the pasta roller to cut it into strips. She hung it over the spokes of the dryer.

"I need to go out to the Orto and pick some fresh tomatoes for the sauce. Maybe you and Hana would like to explore the vineyard?"

RJ untied Hana's apron, then her own, and they followed Tessa outside.

The sun had climbed, late into the morning, the air fragrant with the scent of the grapes, but the heat fell upon her, clung to her.

Tessa headed over to a massive, gated garden with yellow roses climbing the arched trellis beyond the summer kitchen. She pointed to the kitchen as they passed. "We'll make dinner there, with our guests."

Guests? Maybe she meant her and Hana, but RJ's heart gave a thump.

Hana had found another kitten and taken off after it. RJ ran after her, down along the cobblestone pool area, the water so impossibly blue she nearly kept running right off the edge.

But Hana ran past the pool area, descending stone steps, then followed a narrow gravel path past the protective cypress trees.

She vanished past the trees.

"Hana!"

RJ took off after her, found herself in another garden, this one lush with bushes of hydrangeas, more climbing roses, and a pond in the center, with a small fountain in the middle and a string hammock between two trees that listed in the slight breeze. Beyond that, a grove of olive trees shivered in the wind, protecting the garden.

Hana had kept running, down the path that led to the vineyards.

Miles and miles of trellised vines, with tiny green grapes, some with streaks of purple trailed down the hillside as far as she could see. Wide paths ran between different sections, with shelters built into the hillside, maybe to house tools. The sky arched overhead, white cirrus fat and plumpy over the far away hillscape.

And to her left, just down the hill, sat the open entrance to the grotto.

Her feet led her there even as she spotted Hana with the kitty, trying to capture it around a row of vines.

She laughed, and RJ turned to the open grotto.

Wine casks lay on their sides, floor to ceiling, along one side of the arched grotto, the ground smooth and packed. A cool breath stole past her even as she stepped into the shadows, the daylight unable to press in too far. She spotted a cable running along the top of the cave, the electrical line, probably.

Indeed, lights hung along the top, fastened with a long pole.

She started back, wrapped her arms around herself and imagined a pallet on the floor, a young girl carrying polenta.

A voice outside—male—made her turn and she walked out, worried for Hana.

An elderly man sat on a wide pushcart, the kitty in his lap, gnarled hands caressing its ears. She could practically hear the kitty purring. He was speaking to Hana in Italian.

She'd put him in his early eighties, maybe. Tanned face, lean frame, he wore baggy work pants, sandals and a cool linen short sleeve shirt, years of work in his sinewed arms.

A layer of white whiskers suggested an early morning, and when he looked up at her, his eyes blue and curious, she felt like she knew him.

Strange.

"*Vieni qui.*" He patted the space beside him on the cart. Gestured her over.

Okay. She came over and sat next to him. "*Ciao.*" She stuck out her hand. "I'm RJ."

"Umberto." He shook her hand. Then he turned to Hana and held out the kitty. "Bella."

Hana repeated the name.

"This is Hana," RJ said, and Umberto nodded.

He tucked his hands between his knees. Glanced at the grotto, and his smile fell. He shook his head.

"*Bisnonno!*"

The shout came from a younger man, mid-thirties, dressed in jeans, work boots and a collared white shirt with the Mattucci Logo on the breast. "Sorry," he said as he came closer. "My great-grandfather likes to wander off." He came toward the older man, Italian on his lips, a smile, despite the scolding.

Umberto said something back to him and the man looked at RJ. "Why are you in the grotto?"

"The door was open."

"Right. That accounts for it. Sometimes he forgets, or rather, remembers." He reached out and helped the man up. "He thought you were Angelica."

Really.

"I'm Bert. I'm the vinedresser here." He held out his hand.

RJ shook it. "RJ. I'm...visiting."

"Are you with the lunch group? I saw a car drive up."

She got up, looked toward the house. Ziggy?

Or better, York.

"*Pidyom*, Hana," she said and held out her hand.

Hana looked at her, but strangely, obeyed, slipping her hand into RJ's, the kitty under the other arm.

"Nice to meet you Bert," she said and turned toward the path.

"*Mi dispiace! Mi dispiace.*"

She turned, and to her horror, Umberto had his hand over his eyes, tenting them, clearly distraught.

Bert put his arm around the older man, speaking to him softly.

"What's wrong?"

"I don't know. He just keeps saying he's sorry." He looked at RJ. "Don't mind him. He's caught in the past. I'll take care of it."

She paused but hadn't a clue how to help.

"C'mon, Hana."

They headed toward the house, but half-way there, the kitty squirmed away, and took off for the garden.

Hana pulled out of her hand.

"*Ostaroshna!*" RJ called. But really, Hana could hardly hurt herself out here.

She took off running toward the house, up the stairs to the pool area, past the summer kitchen, then out into the driveway.

A man stood with his back to her. Broad shoulders, wearing a hat, his hands in his pocket, talking with Tessa and Santini. Another man had walked away, standing where she had, admiring the postcard. He wore a suit. Dark hair, older. Held himself with a stiffness, as if the travel had taken a toll.

She slowed, her feet scuffing the gravel. Tessa looked up, as did Santini.

And then the man turned.

His face slacked, his mouth opening.

Her too. What—?

Slowly the man smiled, shook his head. And then world-famous action hero, Winchester Marshall said, “Hey Couz. What are you doing here?”

He’d had worse nights, but York had a hard time remembering when.

Roy sat on the hospital bed holding a bottle of water. In the light of day, Roy looked like he’d been dragged by a tractor trailer, the road rash covering his face, his arm, a torn swatch in his leg. No wonder the woman who’d picked them up at oh-dark-hundred this morning had taken one look at Roy and driven them to the hospital.

York supposed he didn’t look much better, his jeans torn, his shirt bloody, part Roy’s part his from one of his stab wounds reopening in his back. By the time the woman picked them up—and he had to give her credit for guts because really, they looked like a couple thugs collapsed by the side of the road—he couldn’t walk a step further.

He’d slept, his head bumping against the window of her tiny, ancient Opel Corsica, his feet against his chest in the back seat while Roy held his arm to his chest and tried not to groan in the front.

York figured they’d put a good ten, maybe fifteen kilometers between them and the mess on the highway, but the woman had to be wondering. Thankfully, he didn’t speak Italian, and Roy only answered in grunts.

She practically pushed them out of the car as they pulled

up to the San Paolo Hospital in Civitavecchia. He'd helped Roy in, set him in the chairs and the nurses immediately ushered them to beds in the ER.

He'd curled up and fell asleep, uncaring at his unwashed, untended state. Hadn't woken until the doctor came in and started messing with Roy's arm.

Apparently, his collarbone was broken. Which, of course, York could have told them—one look at the lump in his shoulder, and he knew.

The docs took Roy away for x-rays and York dropped off again, despite the buzz in his head that maybe he should keep an eye open. He woke again to the prodding of a young, female intern who was checking on his wounds.

"You tore a couple stitches," she said, her accent thick. She was pretty—dark skin, short hair, hazel eyes. More, however, she had gentle hands as she shot him with anesthetic and put in a couple stitches.

"How'd this happen?" she asked as she finished up.

"Car accident. On our way up the coast." Not a lie.

"Terrible. Your friend is pretty banged up."

"He'll be okay," York said and sure enough, when Roy returned, they'd splinted his arm, no surgery, and added salve to his face, his arm and leg.

"Say nothing," Roy said, his mouth a dark line. Roy had no doubt that the gauze on his face would vanish in the hospital receptacle the moment they left.

York had no comment, really, because once the fog of pain and fatigue started to clear, his brain returned to the events of the night before, trying to unravel how Gregori had found their hotel, set a tail on them so fast.

If it was even Gregori.

He didn't know when Roy had placed a call, but the

hospital hadn't even discharged them before a woman arrived, calling Roy's name in the ER.

"This is Ziggy," Roy said, pushing himself up.

York noticed the look of horror she gave him, even as she delivered the typical Italian double-kiss greeting. She was pretty—dark hair, striking brown eyes, and dusky, tanned skin, lean, strong frame. High cheekbones, her hair pulled back in a thick ponytail.

Seemed exactly the kind of woman Roy might partner up with.

"And this is York," she said, turning to him. "You're exactly as RJ described you."

The words were fire, burning through him. He didn't want to ask for details, only, "she's with you?"

"She's at our villa. She's safe. And just fine."

He looked at Roy who nodded.

Okay, so breathe.

Ziggy leaned against the door frame, her arms folded over a pink tee-shirt, a pair of jeans, runners. "Okay, sum up. What happened to make you two look like you were in a road fight."

"A road fight," Roy said. Smiled.

She narrowed her eyes.

"A guy followed us from Berlin, threw a grenade into our car and tried to kill us."

Her mouth opened. Then closed. She drew in a breath. "Okay, now I want it all."

"We don't know much," Roy said. "York met with an old contact, thinking RJ had been taken by someone working for the Bratva. Asked him to nose around. Problem is, York here has a bounty on him. A million Euros."

She gave a face of approval. "That might buy me a nice yacht."

York looked at Roy, who glanced at him, lifted a shoulder. "She's not wrong."

He shook his head.

"So," Ziggy said. "You think this guy had you tailed, and then tried to take you out for the cash?"

Roy nodded.

York shook his head.

"Really?" Roy said.

"I dunno. It's just...yeah, Gregori would sell his own mother if he thought it would make him money, but...I didn't see it in him. He knew there was a bounty on me—he could have had me tailed and taken the minute we left the park. Why set a tail on us, follow us to Rome? No, this was a for hire gig, and I don't see Gregori reaching out to share."

"Then who?" Ziggy asked.

The nurse came in with papers for them to sign.

Roy and York went through the discharge, then followed Ziggy out to a beautiful, BMW Touring wagon.

York opened up the door to the back seat before Roy could grab it and climbed in.

Ziggy got into the driver's seat. "Hungry?"

"I just want to get to RJ."

"I could eat," Roy said. "There's an Autogrill not far from here."

Perfect.

But this time, York ordered an omelet bacon panini, another cup of coffee and felt nearly human when they climbed back into the car.

He leaned against the window, his arms folded, his leg up on the seat, his mind churning over Ziggy's question.

"Who knew you were in Europe?" Ziggy asked as they turned out onto the highway. The sky arched overhead, another gorgeous day, but York just wanted to see RJ.

Confirm that yes, she was just fine, to use Ziggy's words.

Although, honestly, they irked him just a little.

Just. Fine.

He was far from fine.

He sighed. "Our team—the Caleb Group and well, Alan Martin of course, and Ruslan Gustov."

"RJ filled me in on Martin. Who is this Gustov guy? The name sounds familiar."

"Damien Gustov was his brother."

Her mouth opened. Closed. She glanced over her shoulder at York. "You killed him."

"Mmmhmm."

"You think he could have found you in Berlin."

He looked out the window, at the hills and shrubbery along the ditch. "We found your safe house in Heidelberg. What happened there?"

"I don't know. Shooter—nearly took out RJ. Scrubbed me, but we were able to get out."

"Any idea who?"

"No. Long range shot I think because we were on the third floor, a few houses between us. And they couldn't get to us as we escaped."

"So maybe a one-man job. Or they would have flushed you, met you coming out." Roy glanced at her.

"I was careful. But yes, probably a one-man job. Poorly executed."

"Not Martin then. And Gustav is a scientist," York said.

"Someone else, then. Why?"

Silence, and York opened his eyes. Roy had sat up, Ziggy touching her brakes.

A burned Fiat sat in the ditch, pushed to the side of the road.

"Grenade?"

"Good thing York saw it," Roy said.

A cop stood in one lane, directing traffic around a slew of other cops, dressed in black, road patrol. An ambulance was parked on the other side, the doors open, a number of body bags inside.

"Pieces of him?" Ziggy said, nodding and smiling to a cop.

"He had a grenade in his weapons pouch. A small stockpile, actually."

They drove by the Ducati, laying on its side, a cop guarding it.

"Nice bike," Ziggy said. "Shame. Did you get any of the weapons?"

Yes, she and Roy definitely worked together. At least they thought alike.

"We didn't want them traced to us," York said.

"You said you didn't want to be arrested as terrorists," Roy said.

"That too."

They pulled away from the wreckage, then continued up the road, Ziggy putting the gas down. The more miles between them and the body bag the better.

"So, a one-man job. A shooter, probably for hire," Ziggy said. "Okay, who hired him?"

More silence.

"There is one more person who knew you were in Europe," Roy said finally.

York had sat up during their tour of the debris. Now, he frowned. "Um, RJ? The base commander?"

"Winchester Marshall? The guy who stole your reservation, who pulled RJ to a coffee shop where she just so happened to spot Alan Martin. The same Alan Martin who cut you, and kidnapped RJ, not once, but twice —"

"And nearly a third time, in Heidelberg."

York sat back. "Yeah. I know. But...he's an actor, not a spy, not a secret agent. I know he plays one in the movies, but really the guy is about as crafty as Santa Claus."

"Who manages to sneak in and out of a billion houses in one night," Ziggy said. She looked at Roy and winked.

York shook his head, looked out the window. "Okay. Fine. What would Winchester Marshall want with my death. And don't say yacht—he probably has one."

"Maybe it's not about the bounty. Maybe...I dunno. Remember what you said about the CIA using famous people to courier information. Maybe Alan Martin—or the rogue CIA group we talked about—asked Marshall to track you down, set you up."

It didn't feel right. Spit-balled, maybe pieces stuck, but... "What about the plane crash?"

"What plane crash?" Ziggy said as she passed a slow-moving Fiat. Oh, he liked how this woman drove.

"Gustov took down a plane in France—it was full of Marshall's publicity team."

She looked at Roy. "Took down the plane?"

"Yes. He was supposed to be on it, but it had mechanical issues, so he left earlier, on a commercial flight."

"So, they thought they were killing him?"

"Or maybe they deliberately created a diversion. Maybe he was supposed to live," Roy said.

"Still feels wrong," York said. "Killing him would make a big splash. Investigations. Scrutiny. He's an international star—he has fans in China, for Pete's sake."

"Has he been to China?" Ziggy asked.

"Probably," York said.

"Now that feels like something the CIA would be interested in."

A pause as her words settled in.

Then, finally, York said, "But what does it have to do with me?"

More silence.

"We need to find Alan Martin," Roy said. He turned to Ziggy. "I need a phone. Mine blew up in the Fiat."

"You also need a change of clothes and a bath."

He grinned at her, and York just stared at him. Oh brother.

York settled down in the back seat, staring out the window until the world turned fuzzy.

The BMW jerked him awake an hour, maybe more later as Ziggy turned onto a gravel road. He sat up. "Where are we?" They were winding up a hill toward a beautiful stone home, set amidst vast fields of grapevines and olive trees. The sun was high upon the white stone, glinting off the tile clay roof and if he wasn't mistaken, he thought he spotted a pool half-hidden behind cypress trees.

The road dipped down and he lost the view, but — "This is your *villa*?"

"It's a beautiful day to be alive," Ziggy said.

If you lived here, it was.

They pulled up into a large courtyard under the shadow of the three-story stone house. Another house, smaller, sat off to the side. The courtyard was cordoned off by tall cypress trees, beautiful flowers in terracotta planters.

Ziggy got out. "I'll run into town later for a phone and clothing. For now, let's get you guys inside, fed and maybe showered. It's like riding with a car full of futbòl players."

He didn't think he smelled that bad. But maybe.

Instead of heading toward the double wooden door, however, Ziggy led them along the house to the back, through a cobbled corridor, to a pooled area.

He stood, just taking in the view of the pool, the vineyard, the buildings...

RJ.

He drew in a breath, about to shout her name.

But she sat on a chaise lounge, half-turned away from him, wearing a white sun dress, her legs and feet bare, her hair down, blowing in the wind under a wide-brimmed straw hat, holding an empty glass, and...

Laughing. Something bright and high and sweet and it drifted across the pool deck and caught him up, swelled his heart.

And then she reached out and touched the knee of the man across from her.

A man dressed in dark swim trunks, a loose shirt, open to show his waxed, perfect chest, who now turned to her and grinned, also laughing, as if he might be completely charmed be her presence.

And her, his.

Who—

The man got up, reached for RJ's empty glass.

The wind caught his too perfect, thick dark hair, blew his shirt against his frame, and his whitened smile nearly caught a glare.

Winchester. Marshall.

Actor.

CIA mole.

Traitor.

Possibly, assassin.

York stilled, painfully, completely aware of his ripe smell, his soiled clothing, his four-day beard growth, the ache in his back, and the way his jaw tightened.

Oh sure, she was just fine all right.

York strode toward her, unable to think, unable really to respond to Roy's shout behind him. Even unable to look at RJ, who also stood, calling out to him.

He'd worked up a good head of steam by the time Marshall rounded the end of the chaise lounges, two glasses in his hand, and frankly, nothing was left in his head but one thing.

He took Marshall out around the waist, peddled forward, and slammed him into the cool, bright water of the Mattucci pool.

CHAPTER FIVE

This could not be happening.

No. Just...

No.

York was not in the water, wrestling with renowned actor Winchester Marshall, having tackled the poor man in a flat out run across the pool deck.

Hadn't landed with a cannonball splash, fully clothed into the crystalline waters, only to surface and grab the man around the neck, pulling him up—at least he wasn't drowning him.

Still — "York!"

Another shout, behind her, and another splash, water darkening the cobblestones as a man joined the fracas in the pool.

Not Roy, because he ran to the edge wearing—a sling? — shouting at York. Who was now kicking away the second man in the water, losing a battle with Winchester, who had reached up, got a hand between York's arm bar and his neck, started shouting.

Then another splash and suddenly Ziggy—where had she come from—was in the water, launching herself onto the back of the second man.

Lincoln Cash ran to the edge now, shouting and oh, RJ got it.

The second man was one of Win's bodyguards, usually making themselves invisible in the shadows.

"York!" She joined Lincoln and Roy, shouting into the fracas. "Let him go!"

York ignored her, clearly, because he dragged Winchester back, despite the man's bulk, to the stairs, then sat down, the man still in his grip.

But Win got a hand up and smacked York, hard, in the face.

York grunted, but she knew her fiancé.

It would take more than that for Win to shake loose.

Ziggy, meanwhile, had a spider grip on the bodyguard. RJ had seen him before, in France, dark hair, lean and tough. Lake—yeah, that was his name.

Now Lake jerked back in the water and buried Ziggy.

Oh—! "Ziggy!"

She should go in. But what—she wasn't the best swimmer. And—

Ziggy broke free, surfaced and bounced away, breathing hard, her dark hair in wet clumps around her face.

Lake also surfaced, rounding on her, then shooting a glance at York.

Win, the champ, held up his hand, his grip firmly on York's arm, working himself free.

"York! Let. Him. Go!" RJ ran to the edge of the stairs. "What are you doing?"

Win yanked free of York's grip, pushed away and rounded on him, his eyes dark. "What the —"

He left off the last word, but there was no acting in his fury.

He stood, waist deep in the water, his fists balled, breathing hard.

And then everything went quiet as all eyes focused on York.

He hoisted himself up, his wet clothes clinging to his body, glared at Win, then turned and sloshed out of the pool.

Didn't even look at RJ as he stalked away.

Where was he going?

Maybe nowhere. Maybe just away from the chaos of the pool, whatever abysmal judgment had caused him to tackle her famous cousin.

She met Win's eyes. "Sorry," she said quietly.

His shoulders rose and fell, his jaw hard.

So, maybe it was too soon for apologies.

Turning, she ran after York, down the cobblestone steps to the flower garden.

He was facing the water fountain, sopping wet, his short dark-blond hair standing on end, his jaw tight as he stared out, past the olive trees, to the horizon. Or wherever. Maybe he was caught inside a vision of whatever had made him take down Win.

"York?"

"What is he doing here?"

He didn't look at her, just stood, his fists tight, his chest rising and falling. He looked rough, frankly. As if he'd been in another *tussle* as he called it, a bruise on his chin, lines under his eyes, ripped jeans. Clearly, he'd had the same rough five days she'd had.

Maybe rougher.

"He's scouting a film based on a memoir. It's located here, so he came to see if they could film on location."

She'd asked Win the exact same question—although with more cheer, and minus the hint of accusation and suspicion—when he'd arrived, after he'd turned and called her Couz.

And after the embracive hug he'd swept her in, as if they were old friend. No, *more*--family. He looked every inch the fabulous movie star, with the white linen attire, the aviator sunglasses.

"I'm thinking about directing a movie. An epic World War Two movie about the Italian resistance." He'd then reached into the car and grabbed a worn paperback. "It's a memoir by the woman who used to own this estate."

Huh. "I'm reading it right now, actually."

"Then you know why —"

"Don't tell me." She held up her hand, then glanced at Tessa who smiled at her.

His bodyguards had arrived in a car right behind him, but by then Win had started the tour of the grounds with Tessa and Santini.

She tagged along, learning much of what she already knew about the history, the architecture of the summer kitchen, even the darkened grotto which they illuminated with a giant switch on the wall. Indeed, lighting hung from the ceiling deep into the tunnel.

"Of course, if you keep going, that's where you'll find the chamber where the Jews hid." Tessa said. "There's a hidden doorway on the far end, after the bend, where they sneaked in and stayed on their way out of the country."

So that's what Angelica was hiding. The Mattucci family were conductors on their own Italian resistance railroad, secreting their Jewish countrymen out of Italy.

Tessa had fed them a lunch *al fresco* on the massive outdoor table, the wind blowing the sheer curtains affixed to the corners of the portico. She filled up on mouthwateringly fresh pasta in a sausage and creamy tomato sauce, with crusty focaccia seasoned with rosemary, a tomato and burrata salad.

After lunch, Tessa had found Hana a child's swimsuit, and

offered RJ a closet filled with hand-me-downs. RJ picked a white sun dress, then went outside to watch Hana as she splashed in the pool, just her feet in.

"Can you swim, Hana?" she'd asked, and Hana had shaken her head. But the little girl did seem happier.

Maybe Tessa was right. Time. Love. Patience.

And then maybe they'd have answers.

Win had joined them and held a sheaf of papers, tacked together with big shiny brass tacks. He showed her the screenplay to *Bring Me Home.*

She'd paged through it, but really, she didn't want to know the end, so instead she asked him how he was, really.

That's when she got the lowdown of the plane crash that had killed his publicity team. "It was horrible. I would have been on the plane had Lake not suggested we go on a commercial flight. I had a meet and greet in Rome to get to." He had looked away, and she didn't think the glaze of his eyes was acting. "I didn't know the team well. But...seven people." He swallowed. "I canceled the rest of the press tour. It just didn't feel right. Thankfully Tessa and Santini had room here, so we extended our stop over a couple weeks until I need to be in Berlin for a commercial shoot, and a publicity event."

Then, he asked her about her family, their home in Montana, and she detailed her brothers, their crazy lives—Knox, who raised bulls for the rodeo market, bodyguard Tate, Ford, a SEAL, Wyatt a national hockey star, and her mom, newly remarried, living on their ranch.

She didn't know what he'd said that had made her laugh, but she remembered him taking her glass and then—

Splash.

Now, she just stared at York, who simply breathed in and out, as if assessing her answer about Win.

"York, why—"

"Don't you think it's strange that Alan Martin found you—us—in Paris?"

She blinked. "I...um...wait. Do you think Winchester Marshall is in cahoots with Alan Martin? Seriously? York —"

"Yes! No. I don't know, okay? It's just too coincidental that he's here. With you. *Again.*" His blue eyes poured into her, searching, as if she might have answers. His chest continued to rise and fall, so much emotion on his face she didn't know how to read it.

Except, maybe, "York. I'm okay. We're okay. It's just a weird coincidence that can be explained. Winchester Marshall is not trying to kill me or you or..." She took a step toward him, put her hands on his wet shirt, the warmth of his skin seeping through it to her skin. "He's just an actor. Not a real spy."

York's mouth tightened.

Then, he closed his eyes, as if the entire situation pained him.

Oh. York.

She slid her arms around his neck and pulled him close. Holding on, her eyes filling. "I'm so sorry I left you." Her voice shook, and she couldn't help it. "I'm so sorry. I thought..." She backed away, looked at him. "I thought I'd be right back."

Only then did she notice that he hadn't moved. Hadn't put his arms around her. Now, he swallowed, and something terrible entered his eyes.

And his words right before the kidnapping, the terrible event in Sicily that ended with him in the hospital, the words spoken at their hotel rose to haunt her. *We keep living this life, and it will turn on us. It will find us. And it will take you from me in the most horrific of ways. And I can't stick around and watch that.*

And then he'd told her he was leaving.

Sure, she'd run after him, but he didn't know that, did he? Didn't know that if she had to choose...

Him. She'd choose him.

"RJ—"

No. Not again. RJ wrapped her arms around his neck and kissed him. A full on, *I'm sorry, I need you, I missed you, please believe in us* kiss.

The kind of kiss that probably stunned him because he didn't move for a second, maybe two. But she didn't care. She pulled herself against him and urged him back to who they'd been. The epic adventures of RJ and York.

Maybe now, even better.

Then, slowly, he softened his mouth, responding, kissing her back.

And oh, York knew how to kiss. In a second, he caught her up, his arms around her waist, pulling her off her feet, holding her there as he dove in with his touch. Hungry, desperate, and heating her through to her bones, her core.

He tasted of coffee and maybe adventure, but also the amazing, safe, consuming man who she could cling to without fear.

The world just dissolved around her. *York.*

Her entire body trembled with the power of letting go, of surrender to his embrace and when he finally lifted his head, met her eyes, he was breathing hard, his eyes thick with desire.

She smiled.

He released a sound, deep inside, part growl, part acquiescence. "Ruby Jane. You are going to be the death of me."

"No. Not anymore. I've learned my lesson."

He cocked his head.

Maybe because yes, she'd said that before, but this time— "I never again want to look out into the dark sky and wonder where you are, and if you're alive. Never want to be more than a phone call away from you. Never want to think that you might...might think that I don't love you."

He blinked. Then, finally, finally, he smiled.

And it was sunshine, right to her soul.

"Do you...do you still have my ring?"

He nodded and reached into the front pocket of his jeans.

How it remained untarnished, she hadn't a clue, but there it was, still gorgeous. A beautiful vintage two carat white gold solitaire, with tiny diamonds in the cradle.

"York —"

"Just put it on your finger and keep it there."

"You're so bossy." But she held out her hand for him to put it on her finger.

"I should put a tracker in it."

She looked at him. "No need. I'm not going anywhere."

He smiled again, a softness in his eyes that made her want to weep. "Not without me, you're not."

Then he kissed her again. Sweetly. Firmly.

Because yes, they were back.

"Now," he said, as he let her go, and took her by the hand. "I could use a nap."

So maybe he'd overreacted, just a little.

Twenty-four hours after his epic taken down of Mr. Beautiful, York could still feel it in his bones. Sure, he ached a little, but really, the rush of fury, the taste of justice kept him terribly aware of how easily he could reach into the person he'd been.

Revive the Bird.

The thought could catch him up, wrap around him, tighten his breath.

No. He was going home. With RJ.

To the life he'd planned for them.

He just needed to make sure he didn't bring the Bratva's bounty with him to their tiny, safe town of Shelly, Washington, a tidbit he'd also left out on his account of their car accident. Sure, they'd been run off the road, but they didn't know why and yes, it was a lie, a big lie. But the last thing he wanted RJ to worry about was money on his head.

A bounty. Which meant assassins stalking them. And yes, it was selfish, but he just needed a whole minute to get his feet under him.

To figure it out, pivot and attack it head on.

He would tell her the truth—really. As soon as he had answers.

And until then, he was just fine letting himself breathe a little, take in the fresh air of the Tuscan countryside, the crisp piney scent of the towering cypress, the earthy fragrance of the grapes, the scent of roses that climbed up outside his window.

He came out of the bathroom of his third story room, steam following him out and stood at the window, a towel around his waist.

Yes, here, at the Mattucci estate, he could feel his heartbeat slow—the nap helped, of course—but last night, at dinner in the summer kitchen, as Tessa, their hostess, had called it, he'd sat under the array of stars that cast upon the glorious skyscape and told himself to calm down.

RJ wore a navy-blue smock—a sort of wispy floral dress, her hair down, windblown, her skin tanned, and she'd never looked more beautiful. The ring on her finger sparkled in the moonlight, and she wove her fingers into York's as she laughed at some story Santini told.

He barely looked at Winchester, not sure what to add onto his crisp apology.

Win had shrugged, then smiled and said, "Nothing my stunt guys haven't done to me!"

Ha. Ha. Ha.

But York had been serious, at least for a moment, and he knew he'd scared Winchester. A man didn't struggle that hard, without precision, if he wasn't panicked.

So, yeah, he'd overreacted, and only RJ's voice behind him, and maybe Roy's, from the side of the pool had brought him back to himself.

To the man he wasn't, not anymore.

He stopped by the mirror over the bureau, checking on his wounds—even the two punctures looked less inflamed, so maybe this time out might be exactly what his body needed, too. He pulled on the new clothing RJ had purchased for him yesterday in Lucca while he slept—a pair of cargo shorts, a white collared linen shirt. Flip-flops. Like they might be on vacation.

She'd also purchased dress pants, a pair of faded jeans, a swimsuit, a couple more tee-shirts and a silly straw hat to match her own.

Apparently, for romantic walks in the vineyard.

Oh, he needed to find a preacher because one more star-strewn walk, and stop off in the garden behind the pool, and he might not let her off at her door down the hall.

Who said he wasn't romantic?

He came out into the hallway, the smell of bread rising from the kitchen in the house, and headed downstairs. Tessa was in the kitchen, kneading dough on a floured table.

"What are you making?"

"*Gnocchi*. For dinner."

"I smell bread."

"*Ciabatta*. For dinner."

"Tessa, you spoil us."

"It's in the blood," she said, winking. "I believe RJ is outside, with Hana."

He'd gotten the story from RJ yesterday, before dinner—that Mads was not, in fact, Hana's father, that the little girl did not seem sick, despite being in a cancer hospital in Heidelberg, and that RJ believed she was actually an orphan, kidnapped from Russia.

Which, of course, accounted for why RJ spoke Russian to her.

Hana had made a friend of Roy too, who helped her catch a kitty, then held it as Hana petted it. Funny to see him unwind here, too. He knew Tessa and Santini—spoke enough Italian to converse with Santini by the pool.

Santini had lothario written all over him, but York couldn't help like the guy. He was robust in his acceptance of York, despite the take down at the pool.

Apparently, it wasn't the first time the estate had dealt with commotion—Santini regaled them on the history of the estate through two Italian civil wars, and the occupation of the Germans in World War II.

"They actually took up residence at the house for a few months before the Allies chased them out." He'd refreshed their wine glasses with the house Chianti and then toasted to the brave Italian partigianos who fought for freedom.

Ooh-rah.

"Have you seen Roy?" He'd like to check in, see if Logan had called him. York had still to buy a burner phone, but he guessed that Ziggy might have picked one up for him.

"He and Ziggy went for a walk." Tessa said, glancing up at him. "He comes around now and then, especially after Ziggy lost her friend, Tristan."

Right. Roy had mentioned that. Except he'd used the word, partner.

But Tessa made it sound closer, as in boyfriend.

Really it wasn't his business.

"There's some fresh-squeezed lemonade in a pitcher in the summer kitchen, by the pool and a tray of fruit and crackers, if you're hungry."

A subtle nudge to the fact he'd missed lunch, probably. He hadn't meant to sleep so long.

And yet, his body simply, finally, sank into something and didn't want to let go.

"*Grazie*," he said, and she smiled.

He headed outside, the heat pouring over him. He could probably endure another dip in the pool, this time without the drama.

Even if he found RJ again sitting on the chaise lounge, talking with Winchester.

The actor looked up at York, a hint of wariness in his eyes before he chased it away with a smile.

"York," Win said.

RJ turned and got up. "You okay? I knocked on your door but—"

"I'm fine." He kissed her, touching his fingers to her face.

She nodded as he drew away. "Join us—we're talking about the movie Win wants to shoot here."

Win? Really?

York dragged a chaise over next to RJ and sat down. "What's it about?"

"It's a World War II epic. Remember the story Santini told us last night?" Win was shirtless, his body deeply tanned, and the man hadn't a scar on his perfect body.

Yeah, well, chicks dug scars. York nodded to *Win's* question.

"He left out the part about Fred, the American soldier who saved Angelica's life."

"And others," RJ said. She picked up a worn book from the metal side table, the one with the sweating glass of lemonade.

He should get one of those. "I'm reading the memoir the movie is based on. It's about this wounded soldier who is rescued by Angelica—he calls her Angel—and of course they're falling in love—or at least she is, and he's just realized that her brother is in the resistance."

"Sounds good." Yes, he definitely wanted that lemonade. He got up, even as RJ continued talking.

"It is. He doesn't know it, but hiding in the grotto is a family of Jews needing to escape to the border. But the Nazi's have taken over the village and are looking for a group of partisans who recently blew up a bridge. Her brother is one of them, and if they find him, they find the Jews. And of course, Fred."

"Fred?"

"He's the American soldier. Brave. Handsome." She looked at him. "Reminds me of someone."

He'd poured himself the lemonade, was heading back. "I hope you mean me and not Hot Shot over here."

He meant it as a joke, but Win's face slacked.

Oops. Too soon maybe. "Just kidding, pal." He sat down on the chaise, his mouth in a grim line at the silence that dropped between them. "Listen," he said, not looking at RJ. "I was way... miles out of line dropping you in the pool." At least he hoped so. Sure, he'd been tired, but he still had a lot of questions about the coincidence of Win's arrival. He needed to be better about not letting RJ out of his sight. "I thought you were someone else."

RJ just stared at him. He met her eyes. Yes, he was going with that.

She drew in a breath, then nodded. "There's this guy that's been following us..."

Not a lie, but thank you, RJ.

"Still. I overreacted and I'm sorry."

Winchester glanced at RJ, then back at York. "I guess it's payback for taking your dinner reservation in Paris."

York just blinked at him.

"You were going to propose?"

Oh. Right. "Yeah. You jerk." But he smiled.

Win smiled back.

And so did RJ, and really, that's all that mattered.

"So, you're thinking of filming here? Are you directing and starring in it?"

"No." Winchester shook his head. "I can't be the lead."

"Too much work?" RJ asked, picking up her lemonade.

Winchester frowned at her. "No. It's because Sigfrid Jones was one of the elite Buffalo Soldiers."

RJ shook her head. "I don't —"

"The Buffalo Soldiers were an all-black unit, from the tenth Cavalry Regiment of the United States Army, formed in the 1880's. It's what the Native Americans called them, and it sort of stuck. They were almost singularly responsible for breaking through the Gothic line—the German battle line in Italy."

Win nodded. "It's because of the Buffalo Soldiers, in large part, that Italy was liberated."

RJ looked at York, then Win. "Now that's a story." She picked up the book. "Not only did Angelica fall for an American soldier, but yes, if the Germans had found them, it would have been even more terrible. The Nazi's treated people of color like they treated Jews, as if they were inferior. Fred wouldn't have just been captured—he would have been executed."

"And Angelica with him, especially after —"

"Spoilers!" RJ said.

"It's not a secret that they had a child, RJ," Win said. "Hello, Ziggy?"

"Now you wrecked it for me." She stood up and looked at York. "Try not to go in the pool fully dressed."

"Wait—where are you going?"

"Somewhere people won't wreck the ending!" She shook her head and crossed the patio toward the garden area.

Win grinned. "Such a Marshall."

"You have no idea," York said.

"I might have some. I have a sister, too." Win leaned back in the chair. "Actually, I was about to ask her to unravel the ending for me."

"I'm not a storyteller."

"But you get the story. A soldier, a man dedicated to serving his country, falls in love with a woman who is also dedicated to serving *her* country."

"Yes," York said slowly.

"And sure, they love each other, but they each have a higher purpose. And they put that aside—at least for a moment, but then the war comes back, and suddenly, they have to choose between their hearts or their destiny."

York took a breath.

"My guess is, after what RJ has told me, you get that conundrum."

York stared at him, all his questions suddenly right there. "What has she told you?"

Win took a breath. "Um. Just...that you used to be in the military...Sorry. I didn't mean to jump into something —"

Calm down, York. He took a breath, let the sunshine in. "It's fine. And you're right. As a former soldier, I get it. But RJ is both my heart and my destiny. No choice there."

Win leaned back on the lounger. "Right. But what if you had to choose between saving her, and saving the people she loves?"

"What do you mean?"

"I mean, what if she asked you to save the people she

loved—in Angelica's case, her brother, even the Jews she was protecting, and that meant letting her die—"

"I wouldn't let that happen." York realized how ridiculous that sounded, but, "I would figure out a way to save them both."

A beat. Then Win glanced at him. Sat up. "York, brother, you're brilliant. Who says you're not a storyteller?"

Then he stood up and he walked away, headed for the house.

York watched him go.

He hoped not. Because he dearly wanted to believe that the happy ending he hoped for was back home waiting for him.

And not some kind of fairytale that would break all their hearts.

CHAPTER SIX

Chapter 12/Portami a casa: un ricordo della resistenza italiana

Tory is out again. It is not like I don't know—our house is old, and one can't breathe without everyone knowing, so of course I know he's sneaked out. And with whom.

The attacks are becoming bolder. And, the SS is searching. Just last week they raided the house of Bernatello D'amico, pulled him and his oldest son out into the street and executed them.

Just like that.

In front of Maricelle and her daughter.

We have an informant in our community, and I fear Tory is next.

The moon is up, gilding the vineyard, the Orto, and I can't bear one more moment waiting in the darkness for his safe return.

There must be something to be done—weeding in the garden by lamplight, perhaps.

It is there, rooting out the weeds that will choke my tomatoes, my onions, the peppers, and ripping the invaders from the earth, that I hear the steps.

I freeze because I have heard stories, and not just of the Waffen-SS, but Nazi soldiers who crawl through our hills, even at night. Soldiers who think nothing of taking what doesn't belong to them—food, supplies, rooms, even the women who tend them.

But I am unprepared tonight, lost in my thoughts of Tory, my memories of father, tears upon my face. The man is nearly upon me when I turn.

I barely make him out in the cresting moonlight, but he crouches beside me, puts a finger to his mouth. "Let's go."

My own mouth opens, shock rippling through me. But Fred puts his hand in mine, weaves his fingers through mine and pulls me up.

Still, he stays low.

I'm not sure why, because we are alone—

Then I see it. Lights flash through the trees.

A car is heading up the hill, and Fred must have spotted it from his place in the grotto.

But how did he see me, alone in the garden?

He douses my light, then pulls me away from the grotto, away from the house, into the hills above the house.

"Get down." His voice is low and soft and yet takes command of my body. We settle into a grove of twisted, feral olive trees that we've left to the wild. Silvery leaves and thick, low branches shroud us as we hide, a view of the house below.

I gasp as an SS car pulls up.

Mother is gone. I've sent her to Rome, to be with her sister because she is worsening, and I fear what trouble Tory will—has—brought upon us.

Men emerge—the Waffen-SS, charged with rooting out the partigianos. "They are looking for your brother," Fred says, and I look at him.

The light illuminates his face, his eyes and they hold worry.

"How do you know?"

"He is not as secretive as he thinks. He stores his supplies—wires, C-4, even a radio—in a cask in the grotto."

"Has he seen you?"

Perhaps my words are too loud because he puts a hand around me and pulls me near, whispers in my ear. "No."

His voice, his breath, send a shiver through me despite the warmth of the night. Fred smells of the earth, and perhaps the heat of the day but his embrace is oddly calming.

"Will they find anything in the house?" he asks as the SS push the door in, the stream from their flashlights shining against the panes.

"No. I don't think so."

He breathes out, nods. "We'll hope they don't go to the grotto."

"Your bed —"

"Shh. They won't find it. Or the supplies. But I can't promise they won't find the Janowitz family."

He knows.

Oh—

I must have gasped because his voice is soft in my ear again. "They have three young children. Did you think I wouldn't hear them?"

"They are too loud." I knew they would be too loud. I should have never let them stay, but how does one turn away a family, a mother, her daughters, a desperate father? "I should have moved them, but...I have no one. They took father, and Mr. Giuliani, and the others and hung them. And...now there is no one to take them to the border." My voice is breaking, and I want to stop talking, but all of it simply rushes out. "And now Tory—this —"

I can't look at the house, can't bear the sounds that lift from the dark yard, of dishes breaking.

Please, don't fire the house.

Suddenly, his arms move around me, pull me against him,

holding me to himself. "Shh." His hands are big, strong, and I can't stop myself from sinking into him.

And am suddenly very, very aware of how I am clinging to him, my arms around his strong torso...

I lift my head and see him looking at me.

As if he can read my mind, his gaze goes to my lips, and I want him to kiss me so badly I nod. I know how foolish I am. But right here, right now, he is here. And I need him.

But he shakes his head. "Angel, I...this..."

"Please." Oh, my voice betrays me, but I let my word linger. "Please, Fred."

I don't know who I am in the moment. Not brave, but perhaps courage is rising inside me because suddenly I'm tired of hiding. This man has sparked something deep in my soul, and although this also frightens me, I thirst for it.

I will call it hope.

"Angel," he says, and I know he will deny me, so I lean up and press my lips to his.

They are salty, probably from the orzo and fish I brought him for dinner, the crusty bread, fresh butter.

At first, he does nothing. No movement, just stillness.

I might also be shocked for I'm not a woman who has shared many kisses. Delamico, when I was sixteen. And Santini kissed me a year ago, right before he was conscripted. I made him no promises, not even then.

And especially not now as suddenly, Fred gives way for me. His mouth softens and opens and I feel the taste of his tongue, tasting my kiss.

His strong hands find my hair and tangle them in my tresses and I slide my arms up to cradle his shoulders and push myself against him, holding on as he deepens his kiss. His arms cradle me even as he presses me back, onto the soft ground, the olive trees a canopy above us.

I have forgotten the Germans. Forgotten Tory, mother, father, the Janowitz family, even the terrible war within and beyond the vines. I am just here, now, holding on, surrendering, comforted, comforting.

Perhaps I do not know what love is, but in this moment, I feel that it must be that feeling of knowing you are safe. Knowing you have found someone who will see you, find you, accept you, protect you.

Knowing that, when he leaves, he will take everything of you with him.

And without him, you will be bereft.

"So?"

The voice ripped RJ out of the story, and she looked up, trying to gauge just how much heat pressed her face.

"Have you gotten to the good part yet?" Ziggy stood in the garden in a pair of shorts and a tee-shirt, her hair braided. Roy stood with her, smiling.

RJ closed the book. "I...um —"

"She has," Ziggy said to Roy.

He raised his eyebrows.

RJ sat up, swinging her feet over the edge of his hammock. "You've read this?"

"Twice," Roy said. He was healing, she could tell by the way he moved. Clearly the walks with Ziggy helped.

Now, he came over to the edge of the fountain, and sat on the basin. "What people will do for love —"

"Please. Spoilers!" RJ held up her hand. "What is it with you people? Please, keep things from me."

Roy laughed. "If that's the way you want it."

"Well, not everything. I mean—tell me the truth about life, lie to me about the ending."

"Why?"

"Have you not met me? I want the adventure of the read."

Ziggy sat down next to Roy. "Even if it doesn't end the way you want it to?"

"For Pete's sake."

Roy laughed, then winced.

"Are you hurt?" RJ said.

"I think I might have bruised a couple ribs bailing out of the car."

What? "What do you mean, bailing out of the car?"

Roy stilled, look at Ziggy, back to RJ. "Um...didn't York tell you about the accident?"

"Yes. He said that some guy forced you off the road..."

"With a grenade!" Ziggy said.

Everything inside RJ went cold. "A...what?"

Roy sighed. "It wasn't an accident, RJ. It was an assassination attempt. The guy followed us from the airport—actually, from Berlin, but the point is, he didn't succeed —"

"The point is that I know nothing of this!" RJ clasped the book to her chest. "Start at the beginning."

Roy swallowed, drew in a breath. "Maybe York doesn't want —"

"I don't care what York wants. Stop protecting me."

Roy drew in a breath. "York met with an old Bratva contact in Berlin. He told him that there's a bounty on his head, and now that we're poking around Europe, people—mercenaries, probably—are trying to collect."

She just stood there, hollow, staring at Roy.

A bounty? "Who puts a *bounty* on someone?"

"We called Logan yesterday, and Coco is trying to find out."

RJ sank back into the hammock. "So, York is being *hunted*."

"You're safe here, RJ. No one will find him."

She stared at Ziggy. "You don't know that."

"The man who followed us is dead," Roy said, no emotion. "And no one knows where we went."

RJ looked away, her eyes burning. "Did York kill him?"

Roy said nothing.

Oh.

The sun hung high, barely a shadow cast into the garden. Her skin baked, her bones tired.

"I can't believe he didn't tell me."

A beat, then, "He probably didn't want to worry you," Ziggy offered.

RJ looked away. "He's reverting back to the spy I met in Russia."

"He'll always be the spy you met in Russia," Roy said. "The man you fell in love with. It's in his bones."

Yes. And that man thrilled her, sparked the person in her that wanted to be more. But recently... "I just thought he wanted a different life."

"Is there a different life?"

"One without people trying to kill you? I think so."

"Regardless of what we do, we all die," Roy said. "The best you can do is make something of your life while you're here. That's what York is doing. What I'm trying to do." He looked at Ziggy then. "Do the job put before us, whatever that is."

Ziggy nodded.

RJ ran her hand over the book in her lap. "And what is my job?"

"You have to figure that out," Roy said. He got up. "It's what Fred, and Angelica had to do. Keep reading." He winked. "No spoilers."

He walked out of the garden, Ziggy beside him.

He'll always be the spy you met in Russia.

RJ looked at the book. Perhaps I do not know what love is, but in this moment, I feel that it must be that feeling of knowing you are safe. Knowing you have found someone who will see you, find you, accept you, protect you.

Yes, York loved her. Protected her. But—and she heard Roy and Ziggy—he'd lied. And how was she supposed to build a life with a man who lied to her?

She got up and headed out of the garden, fury in her steps, filling her chest.

Someone had thrown a grenade into his car and he....

It was just a stupid accident.

Jerk. Oh—

Laughter. High and sweet and laden with joy. It seasoned the air as she climbed the steps to the pool deck.

Stopped.

York was in the pool. More, he was in the pool fully clothed. Or at least with his shorts on. He'd stripped off his shirt, his body scarred from years of trouble, but still strong, sinewed, his arms nicely muscled.

But most importantly, he was *playing* with Hana. Or at least holding her up as she kicked in the water.

Hana didn't swim. But maybe, with York, she did. Because she knew he'd keep her safe.

RJ froze.

This man has sparked something deep in my soul, and although this also frightens me, I thirst for it.

She was just like Hana. Thirsting to swim, but to be safe, too.

No wonder he hadn't told her. He hadn't wanted to scare her. To be anything but her protector.

Oh, York.

He should have told her. But after the wounds she'd left in their relationship...

Fine. The fury drained out of her as she watched him hold

Hana parallel to the water, teaching her to kick, keeping her afloat.

But Angelica's words stirred inside her. When he leaves, he will take everything of you with him. And without him, you will be bereft.

Well, then she simply wouldn't let anything happen to him. Protection worked both ways, bub.

She walked by the pool, glancing at York, at Hana.

He lifted a hand. "Join us, RJ. The water is amazing."

"I'll go change," she said. "Some of us can't swim in our clothing."

He laughed, and it was like the sunshine sprinkling into her soul.

"I'll be right back." Then she headed into the house to call Coco. She hadn't been a CIA analyst for nothing.

Time to figure out how to save the man she loved.

He could too easily get used to this life.

Sunbaked days, followed by star strewn dinners by the pool, nursing a glass of house Chianti, an amazing spread of salumi, cold salmon and goat cheese to start, followed up by risotto, or fresh-made pasta, maybe a second course of lamb chops or veal, and a finale of tiramisu or pistachio panna cotta. And sure, he had to put up with Winchester Marshall's non-stop stories, musings about location shots, or worse, stories from on-set escapades as Jack Powers.

York wanted to give him a real-life version of hard truth, but what would that do?

Besides he didn't want to give Winchester a reason to avoid him, start hiding. He needed the man close.

Now, Winchester sat at the end of the table, his bodyguard —a guy named Lake—seated next to him. He'd regaled them with a story about Chris Hemsworth, making fun of his accent, and a few of his crazy stunt-fails, and had the entire table—well, at least Ziggy and RJ—laughing.

The remains of dinner sat on a board in the middle of the table—a mouthwatering fig and prosciutto pizza with red onions, arugula and goat cheese, baked in the outdoor pizza oven.

"This is the best pizza I've ever eaten," Roy said as he finished his final piece and pushed his chair back, picked up his wine. He raised a glass to Tessa. She wore a flowing white dress, her hair pulled back in a scarf.

"Agreed," Win said. "*Grazie.*"

She pressed her hand to her heart and bowed. "I hope you all saved room for cannoli." She got up.

Santini took her hand even as she moved away from the table. "She keeps me fat."

Hardly. The man was lean and tan, although admittedly, York had yet to see him work out. Or even work, period.

Then again, York spent most of his hours by the pool...or rather, in the pool. He was turning into a sort of manatee with the hours he spent playing with Hana.

She'd come alive since that moment she'd fallen into the pool. Scared him to death, the splash, the scream.

He'd gone into the water without a second thought, yanking her up. She clung to him, her skinny legs around his waist, her arms gripping his.

"*Vso horosho,*" he'd said in Russian. Everything's okay. He said it again, and she leaned back and looked at him, her blue eyes wide.

"Do you want to learn to swim?" he'd asked without thinking.

She'd nodded, then, and his fate was sealed.

Half play, half instruction, but every day she became more confident in the pool.

And sneaked into his heart. Now, she sat next to RJ, coloring a picture—a fish, a cat, a pool, a house.

RJ also held a crayon, coloring the sun, creating the vineyards in the background. She wore a sweet smile, probably didn't even know it, and in a blink, he saw it—

Their future. Children, seated at a large table, him at the grill, or maybe he'd make his own pizza oven, RJ hollering at the boys to stop wrestling, maybe braiding a little girl's hair like she did for Hana this afternoon.

Yep, he was smack in the middle of Never Never Land. Of his own personal pocket of happily ever after.

But it was fake, wasn't it? Because even as RJ looked over at him, grinned, his words to her—no, his lie to her—turned into a hard ball in his chest.

He should have told her the truth about the attack. The *bounty*.

Because every day that he didn't, the lie grew.

And Coco still didn't have any answers.

"Cannoli, and then it's bedtime, young miss," Tessa said. She'd taken over the care for Hana, who seemed to lean into her like she might be her grandmother, or at least wished it.

Tessa put the tray of round, chocolate covered, cream filled desserts on the table, then handed one to Hana. She held it in both hands as she ate it. "*Vikoosna*."

"Tasty," RJ translated for Tessa, who nodded, winked at Hana.

She beamed around a mouthful of food.

"These are fantastic, Momma," Ziggy said.

"RJ helped make them." Tessa sat down. "She's turning into quite the chef."

"Hardly." RJ laughed. "I can follow directions, that's it."

"That's the start. And then you figure out the rest as you go." Tessa picked up her coffee, made strong, but without caffeine.

RJ was cooking?

York couldn't stop looking at her. The way she held her own coffee cup in both hands, her eyes so impossibly blue under the starlight, the flickering candles in the middle of the table. She wore a light-blue shirt, a pair of jeans shorts, her legs tanned. Her ring sparkled on her finger.

Something about her had changed since they'd found each other again. An easiness about her, and he dared to hope that maybe, hopefully, she'd started to see their future, also.

The life they could have, if they reached for it.

So yes, he'd made the right decision in keeping the assassination attempt to himself. He'd tell her after they cleared the bounty from his head.

"How's the book, RJ?" Ziggy said. "Have you finished it yet?"

RJ put down her cup. "Don't start. So much crying. So, Meyer, the German SS officer—I think she calls him the Obergruppenfüehrer, has moved into the house with his staff, so she's in constant danger. And her brother has gone into hiding. But worse Fred is going to take the Janowitzes to the border, try and get them to safety."

She leaned forward. "Fine. Just tell me. Does he live?"

Ziggy raised an eyebrow.

"He *has* to come back to her. If he doesn't..." She drew in a breath. "Frankly, I don't know what to root for—I hate that he's leaving her, but if they're found, then they all die. There are no good options." She looked at Winchester. "You have to give them a happy ending, or the American audience will kill you. It can't be another *Somersby*."

"Oh, that movie," Winchester shook his head. "I saw it when I was a kid, and my mother left the room sobbing. I don't see the big deal. The guy chose honor —"

"He impersonated a criminal and was hung for it!" RJ said. "He should have told the truth, and let the shrapnel fall."

"Then his wife would have lost everything, his child would have been illegitimate, and the land he'd given to the freed slaves rescinded." Win leaned back. "Sometimes honor is the happy ending."

"Hear, hear," Santini said.

RJ looked at him. "Seriously?"

"Sure. Why do men go to war?"

"It might start out as honor," York said quietly. "But in the end, it's for the man—or woman—next to them. It's for the sake of, well, love, I guess. Love for your fellow man, or again, woman."

Tessa smiled at him. "Well said, York. Love, in the end, is the most powerful emotion made. Look at what God's love did for us."

He looked at her, then nodded, smiled. "Yes. Love is hope. Love is salvation."

"Yeah, and love is truth. Which is what Jack Somersby should have done. Tell the truth instead of breaking all our hearts." She turned to Hana, switched to Russian. "Okay, kiddo, let's get to bed."

Hana sighed but nodded.

"I'll take her," Tessa said and rose, holding out her hand.

Hana took it, smiled up at the woman.

"She's come a long way from when we...I don't know what to call it—rescued? Kidnapped her?"

"I think rescued is the term," York said. "She told me that she was kept in a room at the hospital and that a doctor would come and visit her, take her blood, and that they would feed her, but it feels like they were doing some tests on her."

"What kind of tests?" Roy asked.

"I don't know. But I think it's safe to say that Mads wasn't her father. They were using her. The question is...why."

"Mads certainly used her to trick me into going to Germany," RJ said. "Any news on the whereabouts of Martin?"

York had told her about his meeting with Gregori—had simply left out a few details.

"No," he said now. Truth—Gregori hadn't called him. But the last thing York was going to do is alert the man to the fact he'd survived the attack.

What he really wanted was a short but to the point *tête-à-tête* with the man. Without RJ knowing, of course.

Which only made him look away, the fist again forming in his gut.

"It makes me nervous," RJ said. "He's up to something and we need to figure it out."

York looked at her—oh no—

"Together," she added. Then put her hands on his. "Or we let Roy handle it—after his wing is healed."

Roy looked at her. "Really?"

"I'm not a spy," she said, her gaze falling on Ziggy, then to York. "And I guess it's time I accept that."

"Yes, but you are smart," York said, leaning over to kiss her forehead. "You figured out the EMP bomb in Italy. And before that, the plot against the president."

"There was a plot against the president?" Winchester said.

Oops. There he went, forgetting that there were unvetted ears at the table.

Except, he *hadn't* forgotten. But it seemed that Winchester was authentically surprised, although, he *was* an actor.

Still, maybe not working for the rogue CIA faction behind it all.

Maybe.

"How about a walk," RJ said, and reached for his hand. "Before trouble finds us."

"I think the trouble is standing right beside you," Roy said.

York threw an olive at him.

Roy ducked. Ziggy caught it.

York stood up, grinning. "You think I'm trouble..." he gestured to RJ.

She laughed, sweet and perfect.

Yes, he could stay here forever, the past behind them, the future glorious before them like the vineyard that stretched out into the night.

They walked past the garden, down the pathway, fingers entwined. She stopped before a massive cave, two wooden doors closed. "This is where Fred stayed. There is a tunnel, and it keeps going, all the way through the hill to the other side. That's where he gets the Jews out."

"That's got to be a hard decision—stay and protect the woman you love, or leave."

He didn't know why he said that, just...

RJ turned to him, her eyes luminous in the moonlight. "York. Is there something you're not telling me about...I don't know? The attack? The man you met in Germany? The Bratva?"

He stared at her, but she just looked at him, staring back.

He should tell her. Right, no—no lies. Trust her with—

"York!"

He turned. Ziggy ran down the path, illuminated by the moonlight. "You have a call. Logan Thorne."

"Now?"

"It's only 3 p.m. in Washington D.C. He says he has information on the plane crash—or near crash? The one in Italy?"

Right. He kept RJ's grip in his as they returned. Roy met them in the garden, clearly not wanting Winchester to hear their conversation.

He had Logan on speaker.

"Hey boss," York said, joining the call. "what's up?"

RJ sat on the edge of the fountain. He preferred to stand for bad news.

"Like I told you a few days ago, the passengers of the plane that landed in Sicily were all doctors and researchers from various African countries, on their way to a medical conference in Florence. They met with the new CDC director—Landon Grey, because there's been a case of what looks like smallpox in a village in Nigeria, and they all wanted to get ahead of it."

No wonder Grey was looking into the quarantine procedures at the air base.

"Thing is, Landon is new. And that got us looking into the death of the previous director, a guy named Baumgarten. He was killed in a car accident on his way home. Atlanta traffic—we didn't think much of it. This Grey guy was his assistant and moved into the position pretty quickly."

"Isn't that a good thing?"

"He was recommended, years ago, for the job by Senator Reba Jackson."

Oh.

"You think he's linked to Jackson's group of operators."

"We don't know if he's a target, or a player. But either way, we need to talk to him. We need you to go to Florence, find him and detain him until I can get there."

"You're coming here?"

"Yes. I'll be there tomorrow afternoon. The conference is at the Hotel Bernatello, near the river. It's a beautiful place. I've booked you rooms tomorrow night. And I've cleared you with the secret service. They'll be expecting you and Roy—

"And RJ."

She looked at him. Frowned. But he met her eyes as he leaned into the phone. "If anyone can unravel what he says, figure out fact from fiction, it's RJ."

"I agree. Yes, I booked her a room too."

"And you should add Ziggy to that list, boss," Roy said. "I'm still nursing a broken wing. I could use her backup."

Not like Roy to admit that, but maybe Tuscany had gone to all their heads.

"Will do. See you tomorrow. By the way, Grey doesn't know you're coming, so keep it on the downlow. Just find him and secure him until I can get there."

"Roger," Roy said.

York nearly asked, right then—any word from Coco about the price on my head? The urge pushed him, especially with RJ looking at him with so much...what—gratefulness? No, that wasn't it.

Maybe...trust.

Oh boy.

"See you tomorrow, boss," York said as Logan hung up.

Then, silence.

"I'll go ask Tessa if she can watch Hana," RJ said, getting up. She looked at York again and smiled. "Then I'm going to go pack." She kissed his cheek and walked away.

Roy waited until the darkness had taken her before he spoke. "You sure that's a good idea? To bring RJ with you?"

He shook his head. "But I'm fresh out of good ideas. At least I'll know she's safe."

Roy's eerie silence chased him out of the garden, and right into his bones.

CHAPTER SEVEN

RJ wasn't kidding herself. They weren't here on vacation.

She was here to watch York's back. Even if he didn't know it.

But it felt like vacation. Especially with her view of the Arno river, and beyond that, the ancient Ponte Vecchio, with its tiny shops clinging to the outside, in all colors of yellow, orange and red.

Florence. The name even sounded exotic. They'd arrived early, the cobblestones of Duomo Square still wet from the morning rain. They ate breakfast croissants at a café, then spent the morning touring the Duomo di Firenze, the cathedral built in the thirteenth century. She'd wanted to go into the Accademia Gallery to see the original sculpture of David, but York and Roy headed to the hotel to check in.

Fine. She wasn't exactly suffering at the hotel. Like everything else in Italy, the place dazzled, from the black and terrazzo tiled floors, to the gilded light fixtures to the stained glass windows. She checked into a double room on the fourth floor shared by Ziggy, adjoined with the guys via an inner door. Opulent. The beds were draped with gold bed runners and tasseled gold bolsters. Even the chairs at the tiny round table were upholstered in gold silk, with matching gold-silk drapes. A vase of fresh white roses sat in the center of the table.

RJ glanced into the icy green tiled bathroom with the huge soaking tub. "I might have to take a bath."

Ziggy had dropped her backpack onto the bed. "I'm walking to the hotel with Roy and York. We'll meet you on the rooftop garden after he and York locate Grey."

They'd already received a packet of information from Coco—including the hotel layout, the conference schedule and Grey's room. The hotel wasn't large, eighty guest rooms with only one conference room that held less than a hundred attendees. Coco had even provided the attendee list—less than fifty, all medical professionals, with the focus on global pandemics.

The thought sent a shiver through her. Smallpox. She didn't know much about it, but thankfully the world had a vaccine, right? Still, it paid to be prepared.

The plan was to wait until the afternoon break, then meet him in his room, and detain him until Logan arrived.

Rooftop garden. Maybe the bath could wait.

But really, she should get her head in the game. "Good idea. I'll join you."

Ziggy had pulled back her hair, wore a pair of black leggings, a black shirt, a white blouse over it, a pair of black runners, looking every inch a woman who could handle herself.

RJ wore a sun dress, a hat and sandals. Not exactly ready for trouble.

"On second thought, I'll meet you in the garden."

Ziggy grabbed her key card. "Meet you in twenty." She let herself out and RJ opened her suitcase-slash-backpack she'd picked up on a shopping trip a couple days ago, along with a fresh wardrobe—just a few pieces, but she did own a pair of black pants, sturdy sandals and a sleevless shirt.

She changed, then picked up her new burner phone and checked messages. One from Coco, sent early this morning.

Coco, of course, doing all her work in the wee hours of the morning, when the house was quiet.

I found the contract on York on a site in the dark web. The posting went up the day after you saw Martin in Paris. Two days after he escaped from prison. Be careful. It sounds like York is in the way of something. XO.

RJ sank onto the bed, sorting through the words.

If Coco was correct, the posting went up after York and Martin's fight. Which mean that maybe Martin hadn't expected to see her and York at the coffee shop in Paris.

Coincidence? No. She didn't believe in coincidences.

Martin was there for a reason, and it happened to connect with her random visit to the coffee shop with Winchester Marshall.

She stilled. Winchester. And her words, spoken shortly after York tackled Win into the pool, rounded back on her. *Do you think Winchester Marshall is in cahoots with Alan Martin?*

It did feel weird that he'd simply invited her to join him for coffee, right?

But they were cousins, so not that weird.

Except, he accepted that connection easily. Too easily, maybe, given his fame.

No...Except...

She typed out a return text to Coco. *See what you can find out about Winchester Marshall and his possible connection to Alan Martin.*

She waited, but not dots appeared on the screen, so probably her sister had gone to bed.

RJ got up, grabbed her key and left the room.

She took the elevator, which was about the size of a phone booth, up to the top floor, the rooftop garden.

The building was sandwiched into a long line of ancient five and seven story buildings along the bank of the Arno. She reached the top floor, then needed to climb a set of stairs to the top.

But when she emerged, the skyline of Florence across the Arno greeted her, clay-tiled buildings, church spires tall against the horizon, the late afternoon sun backdropping the tall cypress trees and ancient homes that sat on faraway hills.

The terracotta tiled rooftop hosted a number of café tables and chairs. She found one and a waitress emerged from a nearby beverage carts stand. "*Ciao*."

"Just a lemonade, if you have one," RJ said.

"*Bene*," the woman said. Mid-thirties, brown hair, she wore a Hotel Bernatello apron, a name tag that read Phoebe.

On either side of the hotel rooftop garden rose buildings—one rose another story to a similar rooftop terrace. The other side hosted a small building, maybe an apartment connected to the hotel. And beyond that, another building, its clay roof jutting out even with the garden, that opened to a window to what might be an apartment.

Everything jammed so close to each other, it reminded her of many Mission-Impossible rooftop chases.

Of course her brain had to go there. Good grief. She wasn't going to suddenly run across the skyline of Florence, maybe leap into the deep blue Arno River.

This was real life, not a Winchester Marshall move.

The thought of him gave her stomach a pinch. No, he couldn't be mixed up with Alan Martin. Win was kind, not sinister. He might play a spy, but he didn't seem to have a bone of deceit in him.

She sort of wanted to delete the text to Coco.

A couple more patrons emerged from the stairwell, dark-skinned men who wore lanyards around their necks. She guessed they might be from the medical conference.

They sat at an outside table and also ordered.

Phoebe delivered RJ's drink, in a chilled bottle and a glass, no ice. She uncapped it and poured some into RJ's glass.

"Sandwich?" she pointed to the case of pre-made sandwiches.

RJ shook her head. Maybe they'd score a nice dinner after Logan took Grey off their hands.

The door opened and Ziggy came out onto the patio. She spotted RJ and came over, standing next to the table.

"The guys are on their way up. The lift is so tiny. But, bad news. Grey isn't here."

"What?"

"Yeah." Ziggy pulled out the wire café chair. "We searched the conference. No secret service, no personal secretary. We even went up to his room—I think his is right below the guys' room. Only it has a balcony. We searched it—no go. No suitcase, no toiletries in the bathroom. The CDC director has left the premises."

"Did he check out?"

"Not according to the front desk."

RJ just frowned. "That's —"

"Unnerving."

Ziggy nodded. "When does Logan's flight get in?"

"Around 2 o'clock. He said he'd be here by 3 o'clock in the afternoon."

Phoebe came up to Ziggy. "*Ciao* —"

She never finished her sentence.

An explosion shook the building. The entire structure shuddered, then, the floors cracked around them.

"Get down!"

Ziggy turned over the table, even as RJ reached for Phoebe, yanking her down.

Behind them, smoke coughed up, billowing out over the river.

What—?

"It's a couple floors down, but we need to get off this roof," Ziggy said. She'd crawled over to the side of the building.

"This building is old and made of plaster and sticks—it's going to come down." RJ had visions of 9-11, the buildings imploding, and her at the very top. "We need to get out of here."

Across from them, the two doctors had also hit the ground, holding their hands over their heads. Phoebe was screaming, her hands over her ears.

"Where?" Ziggy said and her face betrayed the worst.

From the doorway that led down to the elevators billowed black smoke.

York.

Oh—

She nearly got up. Nearly ran right to the black smoke. But the last—very last—thing York would want her to do was try and rescue him.

No. She had to get herself, Phoebe, the men and Ziggy off the roof.

Although, honestly, Ziggy could probably manage for herself.

Still—RJ had sat here and gotten the lay of the land. They couldn't scale the high wall—but behind them, they could escape through the next building.

"Follow me!" She got up and grabbed Phoebe's hand. Gestured to the men across from them.

The building continued to shake. "It's going to collapse!" Phoebe yelled.

Maybe, but not until they were off it.

Don't think about York.

She ran over to the apartment attached to the hotel. The windows had cracked with the shudder of the building.

But she'd been right about the rooftop to the next building jutting out. They just needed to climb on the clay tile, get the window open and they could get out.

"I'll go first," Ziggy said, seeing the plan. She had to hoist herself up to the rooftop, and RJ gave her a push, holding up her hand for Ziggy to brace it on.

Ziggy kicked off a couple tiles. They crashed on the street below.

"Go easy. This roof is old, and these things are crumbling beneath me."

Another tile flew off, and Ziggy slid toward the edge.

Phoebe screamed.

Ziggy caught herself on the roof edge, lay prone. "Okay, I'll get to the window, open it, and then you push them up, and I'll pull them to the window."

RJ nodded, but held her hand up in case—what? She was going to catch Ziggy from sliding off the edge and five stories down? Maybe, okay.

Ziggy got to the window, then opened it. Braced her hand on the sill. "Ready."

Behind them, more explosions sounded, the building trembling.

"C'mon, Phoebe," RJ said and made a basket with her hands.

Phoebe shook her head.

"You must go!" This from one of the doctors, who came up

and physically picked her up, pushing her foot into RJ's hands, and manhandling her to the roof.

RJ might have taken a different approach, but it got the woman up and she grabbed Ziggy's hand. Ziggy pulled her into the window.

"You next," said the doctor who'd pushed Phoebe up.

"No—you go!"

She made a basket, but he ignored it and scrabbled up the side. But his feet knocked off a cluster of clay tiles and he slipped, face planting onto the roof. Blood erupted on his face, his nose broken. He clung to the site of the roof panting, whimpering.

"You can do it." Ziggy held out her hand.

He looked up, the blood streaming off him, but grabbed her hand.

Ziggy hauled him in, then disappeared with him into the room.

"Now you," RJ said to the other doctor. He was smaller, thinner, older. Maybe a buck thirty, sopping wet.

He shook his head. "You go."

"No—!" She grabbed his arm, yanked it. "You won't fall—just be careful."

Ziggy appeared back at the window, climbing out. "Let's move!"

A siren whined in the distance, and from the water, a boat sounded its horn.

Please, be okay, York.

She made a basket with her hands, and this man took her up on her offer to help. Ziggy scrambled down the roof, got a grip along the edge and got a hold of his arm to help pull him up.

He landed on all fours on the roof, unable to move, breathing hard.

"C'mon, doc, this roof is going to collapse," RJ said, not sure of her words, but feeling it in her gut.

The man nodded, then reached for Ziggy's hand. She'd repositioned herself at the window and helped him climb up. He practically collapsed on the frame, and she disappeared inside, probably to help pull him in.

RJ dragged over a chair from the table. Put it against the wall. Climbed on, waiting for Ziggy.

"RJ!"

The voice lifted from behind her, across the terrace...

She turned, searching. "York?"

Nothing. But she'd definitely heard her name. "York?"

She started toward the door—

"RJ! Where are you going? The roof is going to collapse!" Ziggy, frantic at the window.

"York!"

"RJ, Come on!"

She turned back, headed for the chair.

And heard it again. "RJ!"

Looked at Ziggy. Then she shook her head and took off toward the billowing black smoke rolling out of the open door.

Not. *Again.*

"You still with me?" He directed his question at Roy, somewhere in the debris-filled darkness of the lift, which had come to a shuddering stop with the explosion.

An explosion that sounded too close, and now with the smoke that billowed in around the compartment, a roar not far away, he guessed that the explosion might be on the floor they'd just left.

Floor three, the same floor as Director Grey's room.

"Yeah," Roy said, but his voice sounded tight.

York could just make him out, and now reached out and grabbed his arm. Roy grunted and he guessed that the man had re-injured his collarbone. But he helped Roy to his feet.

"This entire building could come down," Roy said.

Yeah, he should have listened to the feeling that sat in his gut for the last hour—the fact Grey had left the premises without checking out said he'd either been kidnapped or was on the run.

And if it was option two, someone had tipped the man off.

But right now, all he cared about was getting to RJ. Ziggy had mentioned she was meeting them on the rooftop terrace.

"Let's get these doors open." He braced himself on one side of the door, with Roy grabbing the other.

They pulled, but it wouldn't budge.

"We need more *oomph*," York said, even as the box began to fill with smoke. His eyes had adjusted to the dimness and now saw Roy. He was holding his arm tight against his body.

"Try the open-door button," Roy said

"It won't open mid floor."

Roy tried it.

Just like that, the door dinged open.

Smoke poured in. York hit the deck, Roy next to him. Fire roared in the choking fog.

"Let's get to the stairs," Roy said.

Good idea, but he hadn't exactly memorized the exit map. But maybe Roy had because he headed out, crouched down, into the blackness.

York grabbed his jacket lapel and tucked his nose in it, fighting the smoke, his eyes burning as he followed Roy.

Just a few feet away, Roy opened a door to the stairwell.

Smoke rose through this also, black and lethal, pouring out

of a door below them. But it dissipated in the open door two stories above, out to the roof.

Roy headed up the stairs, York on his heels. They came to the fifth floor, ran out into the landing. The door to the rooftop terrace was open.

The hotel still shook, trembling from the shock of the fire. And in his gut, he knew it was going to collapse. "RJ!"

He didn't know why he shouted her name. But all he could think was—get off the roof! Get off the roof!

And then Roy tripped on something and went down. His shout suggested he hadn't broken his fall.

York looked down.

A body. On the floor was a woman. She didn't look injured but—he pressed a finger to her neck even as Roy found his footing, growling back pain.

"Is she dead?"

"No. But maybe she hit her head with the blast." Indeed, now he saw blood leaking out from behind her head. She wore a lanyard from the conference, probably one of the doctors. He leaned over her, trying to awaken her, but she stayed still.

The building shuddered again. Aw — "RJ!"

Then he reached out to pick up the woman.

"York!"

RJ fairly burst through the open door, like a woman on fire, her eyes wide. "York!"

He wanted to grab her up, pull her tight, but he had another woman over his shoulder. "RJ!?"

She nodded, glanced at Roy. "C'mon! The building could go down." Then she put her arm around Roy and pulled them toward the terrace.

His gut said take the stairs.

But the woman he loved was gesturing to him outside. "Where are you going?"

She glanced over her shoulder. "Trust me!"

Oh wow. But—maybe it was time he started trusting her.

He carried the woman out to the terrace. "RJ —"

She had already helped Roy over to the edge of the terrace where she'd set up a chair. He climbed up it, then onto a clay-tiled roof, kicked off a tile or two scrambling up to Ziggy who waited at a window.

Huh.

RJ had returned to him. She's changed clothes—wore black pants, a black shirt, her hair down, and looked every inch the kind of woman that might run through fire to save someone.

Yes, he needed to start trusting her.

"You got her?" RJ asked as he walked over to the chair.

The woman started to rouse.

"Put her down!"

York set her on the chair, crouched in front of her. The woman's eyes opened, and she stared at York, then RJ—

"You're okay," RJ said, stepping in front of York. "There's a fire in the building, and we need to get out. He'll help you, okay?"

The woman looked at RJ, her brown eyes big, then she nodded, and looked at York.

Probably better than lifting her by himself, but he did most of the work as he got on the roof, then helped her up.

He put his hand behind her as Ziggy grabbed the woman's arms and pulled her up.

Behind her, the rumble from the hotel grew louder.

"RJ, let's go!"

York reached out for her, and she got up on the chair.

Another explosion rocked the hotel. It rippled up through the stories, buckled the roof—

The chair toppled as the roof caved in. Just like that, falling into the story below, rubble and dust coughing up.

Flames broke through.

"RJ!"

She clung to the side of the roof, her feet dangling. "York, pull me up!"

He leaned over, grabbed her arms. "Hang on!"

He pulled her up, fighting for purchase on the roof.

Ziggy came down and helped.

RJ got her elbows on the edge, then pressed up, scrabbling with her feet until she rolled over onto the roof, next to York.

She stared at the sky, breathing hard.

He too rolled over, his heart thumping.

"What is wrong with you two? Get off the roof!" Ziggy had returned to the window.

RJ rolled over and reached for her hand. Scrambled up to the window and dropped inside.

York was right behind her.

For a beat, they just stood, all of them breathing hard—Ziggy, RJ, York and Roy. The others she'd rescued had already left, through the bedroom where they'd landed, out into the small kitchen and living room and into the hallway.

They were probably already out in the street.

Sirens now sounded outside the window.

RJ had gotten scuffed up on her chin and elbows in the fall. He touched her face. "If we hadn't gone with you, we might be trapped inside the stairwell."

She drew in her breath, then simply put her arms around him and pulled him close, breathing hard. He buried his face in her neck.

"What happened?" Ziggy said now. She was looking at Roy's wound. "I think you re-broke it, champ."

"It feels that way," Roy said. "I stumbled over that woman..." He blew out a pained breath.

"What is going on?" RJ said.

"I think it was Director Grey's room," York said. "But who knows. Let's get out of here before the fire takes down this place too."

Indeed, the building, attached to the hotel, had started to tremble.

York grabbed RJ's hand and they found their way out to the hallway.

Other tenants had filled the stairwell, and they followed them out, many holding pets. York kept a grip on RJ.

A crowd had gathered in the street, also, and now he and RJ joined them in watching the fire brigade battle the flames that streamed out of the top half of the luxury hotel. Water arched from two boats in the river, and a firetruck had set up in front of the building, the ladder extended to the third floor where firemen had rescued people from adjacent rooms.

"That's definitely Grey's room," Ziggy said. "I remember the balcony. His room was second from the end."

York ran his hand across his face. "But he wasn't there."

"No," Roy said. "Which only we know. The hotel doesn't know it. And presumably, neither do anyone else."

"Did he know about the threat?" Ziggy asked.

Roy lifted a shoulder.

"Looks like it," RJ said.

Indeed.

Then she looked at York. "Ziggy said you searched the room. Did anyone let you in?"

"We used a key card provided by the hotel staff," Roy said.

"To be precise, we got it off hotel security. When we told the security lead who we were, he recognized us from the list Logan had sent to the secret service. He's the one who told us that Grey's security team had left. He'd been given the card to turn in by the Secret Service leaving the building."

"So, it belonged to one of his Secret Service members?" RJ asked.

"Maybe."

She was staring at the building, watching. Flames turned the top half of the building black, the lower half still relatively unscathed except for the water barraging it.

Conference attendees and hotel guests jammed the street.

"Your room was on the fourth floor?" Roy said.

"Yes. The one that is now in rubble," Ziggy said. She sighed. Turned to RJ. "No wonder you pack light."

But RJ didn't say anything. Just kept staring at the carnage.

"RJ?"

"It's just weird that the room blows up after we arrive here. In the room right below us. What if it has nothing to do with Director Grey and..." She looked at him. "I keep thinking about that bounty."

He stared at her, nonplussed. "You know—" His gaze turned to Roy, who held up a hand.

"Sorry—"

"Don't apologize, Roy. York should have told me." RJ shot York a look.

A beat, then, "You're right. I should have. I just didn't want—"

"To scare me. I get it. Fear not, I'm plenty scared without the bounty bonus round."

Right. He looked at the hotel, the flames coughing from the roof, the upper windows. "That's an awful lot of trouble to try and kill me. Besides how would they collect? You need a body. Pictures, at least."

She drew in her breath so sharply he realized he shouldn't have said that.

"Sorry —"

"Nope. I get it. And I agree. It's just...it makes me nervous."

It made him nervous, too, because RJ's question had him thinking—what if they hadn't been quiet enough last night and Winchester Marshall had found out where they were going? If he was in league with Martin...

Well maybe a body or a picture didn't matter as long as York was out of the picture.

"We need to get back to the villa," York said. "Let's get to the car."

She nodded, and maybe, as usual, she was reading his mind.

He hoped so.

"There goes my bath," she said. "And I bought a very cute LBD for tonight."

Or not.

"My keys are in the room," Ziggy said with a sigh. "Unless you can hotwire a BMW X6."

He longed for the easy days of hotwiring cars. Instead, York pulled out his cell phone.

"What are you doing?"

"Calling Logan. We need a ride."

Two hours later, he sat in the back of an SUV that Logan had rented at the airport, having gotten his message. Roy sat in the front passenger seat, catching their boss up on the recent events—and fails.

RJ sat in the back seat, head down, using Logan's cell phone to search the web and send messages back to her sister, Coco, as she sorted out information about the attack on the internet, and other sources.

Ziggy was leaning forward in the bucket seat, also listening to Roy, adding color where he needed it.

But York's brain was back on Winchester Marshall. The fact that man had known—

"Oh my gosh—Coco is right."

Roy stopped talking at RJ's words. Logan looked up, into the rear-view mirror. His boss—about the same age as York, wore his brown hair clipped short, and a dress shirt, suit pants and tie, ever the representative of the president, although he'd loosened it a bit. And, he'd taken off his suitcoat and hung it on a hanger in the caravan.

"What is she right about?" Logan asked.

He'd once been a SEAL, served right alongside Roy and Hamilton Jones, so he was all about getting the mission objective accomplished, and it showed in his tone, the one on the phone and now as they drove back to the villa.

He was annoyed, frustrated and not a little panicked about Director Grey's whereabouts. Or his affiliations.

"Coco reminded me of an explosion that went off in the hotel room of Senator Jackson during a campaign event in California. The bomb was activated by a radio frequency on a microphone Jackson was wearing. It didn't go off until she was in proximity of the bomb—then the frequency armed the device and it went off a few minutes later."

"Where was the bomb?"

"It was ...I think a vase of flowers that was delivered to her room? I can't remember." She looked at York. "There were fresh flowers in my room. My guess is that all the rooms get fresh flowers every day."

"The bomb is in the vase?" Ziggy said.

"Could be," RJ said.

"But what triggered it?" York said.

"You still have that key card?"

York found it in his back pocket, handed it over. RJ took it, looked at it. "I dunno. It's thicker than normal, and heavier. Almost metallic. I'd need to take it apart, maybe get an x-ray machine."

"We can overnight it to Coco," Logan said. "She can take it apart."

"That came from Grey's security team," York said. "You think it's an inside job?"

"Maybe they didn't know?" Ziggy asked.

"Or maybe they were trying to dispose of the evidence." This from Roy. He wore a grim look.

Ziggy pointed to the cut off driveway to the estate. It sat on the hilltop, bathed in a sort of late-afternoon rose-gold from the setting sun.

"This is beautiful," Logan said.

York still hadn't ruled out Winchester Marshall as a culprit. But as they drove into the courtyard, he spotted Winchester in the garden with Hana.

He stood up and waved, grinning.

They got out, and Tessa came out, wiping her hands on a bread towel. "I thought you guys were staying the night in Florence?"

"It's a long story," Roy said.

"I hope it's okay that we brought a guest," Ziggy said.

"Of course."

York got out as Ziggy introduced Logan to her mother. Hana had filled a basket of tomatoes and came out, grinning at him. "*Prevyet!*"

He crouched in front of her, strangely happy to see her.

RJ joined him. Picked up a tomato. Spoke to her in Russian. "Did you have fun here with Winchester?"

She nodded.

So maybe he wouldn't be taking the guy down in the pool again.

"So, did you enjoy Florence?" Winchester said. "Such a beautiful city."

Still, the night was young.

He followed Hana around to the back, past the pool, then into the kitchen garden where she unloaded her tomatoes onto the kitchen table. Tessa returned to dinner. Santini stood at the grill.

It was like they'd never left.

He sank onto a bench, not sure how to shake off the day. The fact he'd nearly lost RJ, again.

Maybe, her, too, because she came over and slid next to him. Pressed her fingers through his.

"Let's get married," he said.

She looked at him. "I said yes, York. You don't have to ask me again."

"I mean—now. Today —"

"Yes."

He looked at her, and she smiled. "Yes. And then we go home."

Yes.

Logan's phone, still in her hand, pinged. She turned it over. Looked at the text. "Coco found Grey."

Logan had joined them in the kitchen, clearly appreciating the grounds, but his attention went to RJ. Who knew how much he'd heard of their conversation.

Ziggy had disappeared with Roy into the house.

"Where?" Logan said.

"She tagged everything she knew about Grey—his history, education, friends, past locations—he showed up in a tweet." She leaned in, reading from the phone. "It's a picture of him and another man—some professor. Some announcement of him guest-teaching for the day."

"What?" Logan reached for the phone and RJ handed it over. He read it, frowned. "He's in Lauchtenland."

"Where is that?" York asked.

"It's a tiny country off the coast of Germany. The future king just married an American. It was in the news," RJ said.

"According to Coco, Grey attended the school for one semester in his graduate years." Logan looked at them, his jaw tightening. "This isn't good." He set the phone down. "Coco continues to find information on the laptop you found in France, the one belonging to Ruslan Gustov."

Another explosion during which York nearly lost his life. Yes, this was getting old.

"He has on it the itinerary of the Russian General, Boris Stanislov—"

"The general who was nearly assassinated a couple years ago."

"He also has the itinerary of the CDC director."

"Which included this week's conference," York said.

"Indeed. The trip to Lauchtenland was clearly something not on the agenda."

Logan looked at York, then RJ. "Sorry guys. Home is not on the agenda yet. We need to get to Lauchtenland."

CHAPTER
EIGHT

Chapter 15/Portami a casa: un ricordo della resistenza italiana

He has left me.

Of course, we planned it, and it is the only answer.

He cannot stay. The Janowitz family must be led to safety.

My heart does not matter.

I cannot deny that the vacancy in the grotto has left me barren in spirit. Barren of hope.

Fred made me no promises, of course. I refused to let him speak them, put my hand to his mouth when he tried. So, he didn't try. Just held me, enveloped me in his embrace, healed now, strong, capable and I knew in my being that he would make it to freedom.

Perhaps that is enough.

In my mind, I have us wed, have us consummating what we began in the olive grove.

It is my shame that I was not the one who hesitated. "We will not find freedom in our regrets," Fred said.

"I have no regrets," I said.

"You might. And I have vows I've made to God," he said.

His words burned in me, for I had forgotten God.

And until Fred arrived, I feared that God had forgotten me.

Perhaps not. Perhaps it is as my father once said. The Lord is near to those who call on him. He fulfills the desires of those who fear him.

I desire that we grow old in this land of my family, and perhaps that is naive, but war changes things. And I care not what the town of Lucca thinks about Fred's status as an American, nor the color of his skin. I only see that he is mine. And I am his, if not in flesh, in spirit.

"I love you, Angel." Fred whispered the words more than once, into my ear, against my neck, his lips brushing my skin, and they found their way to my soul. "Come with me."

I said no, of course. This land holds me. This land, this family.

Tory.

Someone must protect him. The Obergruppenfüehrer Heinlein has searched the grotto and Fred must have hidden Tory's equipment well because they turned up nothing. But Tory has not returned, either, from his last midnight escapade and I fear the worst.

But by day, I tend the vines, with Arturo and Bertie, and prepare food for the Obergruppenfüehrer and his men, and lock my door at night and pray.

I pray that Tory is safe.

That this terrible war will end.

That Fred will return to me.

I pray for miracles.

RJ savored the rich black coffee, eying another piece of soft bread, trying to focus on Logan as he spelled out their mission, all while Angel's story played in the back of her mind.

That, and York's intoxicating question. *"Let's get married. I mean—now. Today —"*

Yes.

"We know he's left the Delafield Hotel in Port Fressa. Checked out this morning," Logan was saying

They were seated around the kitchen table, the morning sun just barely gilding the terracotta floors. Tessa had left them for the garden, having already served them a breakfast of baked eggs and crusty bread, fresh blackberry jam.

Winchester and Lincoln Cash and their detail had left to scout Lucca for possible movie locations.

York poured himself a fresh cup of coffee from the press in the middle of the table. He wore a blue dress shirt, cuffed around his forearms, a pair of jeans, his blond hair tousled after a morning shower. He hadn't, however, shaved, his razor left behind in Florence.

Logan helped himself to one of Tessa's fresh blueberry muffins. "Coco confirmed the source of the explosion in the hotel, a bouquet of flowers in the suite, delivered that morning, so I think your analysis is on the right track, RJ. Something set that bomb off, something designed for the director, possibly when he returned to his suite at the lunch break." Logan said. He nodded at RJ. "Good job."

She nodded, back, but York's voice was in her head. *"And then we go home."*

She hated how much she wanted that. But yesterday's near miss had found her bones.

Her heart.

She was with Angel. If she were honest, the desire for adventure had burned out of her over the past two weeks. She simply wanted York alive, whole, and home.

"Thankfully—and we're not sure how—but Grey left his hotel room with an old friend from Lauchtenland the night before last. He wasn't even in Italy yesterday. We checked into the Tweet—it originated from the account of Arlo Fletcher, PH.D. of contagious diseases. He was at the conference too. Grey guest lectured yesterday at Haxton University, where he once spent a semester. We think that's where he and Arlo met. In fact, they've had a number of meetings over the years, and this isn't the first time Grey had guest lectured. It seems to be a pattern—he pops into Haxton, and then spends a weekend at the Royal Lodge, near Hadsby Castle, in the Highcrest Mountains."

He handed them a map of Lauchtenland. "It's a small island country off the coast of Germany, bordering the small island country of Brighton and the Duchy of Hessenberg. It's ruled by the House of Blue, Queen Catherine on the throne. Ironically, Grey is on the guest list of the tri-annual Queen's Garden Dance this weekend, the Rosendans, at Hadsby Castle."

RJ looked at the map, printed out in black and white. Mountains to the north, the main city, Port Fressa in the south.

"So, he was on his way to Lauchtenland after the conference?"

"Apparently. But he left early," said Logan.

"Has anyone gotten a hold of Grey?" Roy asked.

"Not yet, but we do know that he checked out of the Delafield Hotel where he was staying. My guess is that he's on his way to the Royal Lodge." Logan folded up the map.

"And we are too," Roy said. He wore a new sling but looked a little gray today.

"Yes." Logan said. "And so are you."

"Same mission objectives?" York asked. "Find and detain Grey?"

"And protect him. Until we sort out if he was the target, we need to assume the worst."

"What should we do about Hana?" RJ asked, glancing at

York. She didn't know why, but the little girl seemed her—their—responsibility.

"My mother will watch her until you get back."

Until they got back. York nodded, however, as if reading RJ's mind. "We won't be long."

Huh. But she slid her hand into his under the table. He squeezed it.

Oh, she wanted to believe him.

Logan looked at Ziggy. "We could use your help, if you want to join us?"

Ziggy made a face, shook her head. "I'd like to, but I have my own mission." She glanced at York. Nodded.

RJ frowned.

It bothered her so much that she cornered Ziggy just before she left, knocking on her bedroom door.

Ziggy was packing, her hair back in a dark braid, wearing her leggings, runners and an athletic shirt. "Where are you going? And what does it have to do with York?"

The woman zipped up her backpack. "York asked me to check on someone —"

"Someone connected with the bounty on his head?"

Ziggy's mouth tightened.

Oh, she knew it.

Ziggy drew in a breath. "Any word from your contact?"

"Just that the contract went up on the dark web the day after we saw Martin in Paris. So, my bet is that Martin is the originator."

Grabbing the backpack, Ziggy pulled it onto her shoulder. "I'm just going to ask some questions. I'll let you know what I find out."

"Even if York doesn't?"

Ziggy stood at the door, her hand on the handle. "He still hasn't told you any of the details?"

RJ shook her head.

"He's probably trying to protect you."

"And trying to protect himself." She shook her head. "Please keep me in the loop."

"You two are so alike," Ziggy said. "Stay safe." Ziggy headed out the door.

Ziggy's words still clung to her six hours later when they touched down in Lauchtenland.

Maybe they were. York was passion and risk and courage. But he was also home and family and commitment.

Yes, it was time for them to get married.

Before, like Angel, she lost the man she loved.

Logan had rented a car for them, and they traveled the three hours north up the west coast of Lauchtenland, along highway one, past the old towns, mixed with new architecture. They passed Perrigwynn Palace, the royal residence of the House of Blue, and finally came to the hamlet of Dunholm, with old town facing the quay, off Centre Street, the newer part of town past a row of low buildings, and the Centre Park to the east. The beautiful Highcrest Mountains rose in the distance, green and lush.

They wandered through the old hamlet, paved with cobblestone, past thatched roofed shops and Victorian lamps and finally found themselves at a public brewhouse called the Belly of the Beast.

Roughhewn beams, a stone floor and all the aura of legacy filled the pub, the conversation rich with local dialect, short-handed speech.

RJ and York shared a basket of fish and chips, and York had a pint, while RJ stuck with water. Logan and Roy dove into bangers and mash.

They finally arrived at the resort as the last of the sun hung over the mountains to the west, casting golden rays into the valley below.

The Royal Lodge was built into the side of a hill, with wide ski runs leading down to the A-frame Chalet that spanned the base of the hill.

Built with stone wrought from the hill, and thick timbers, the chalet rose three stories, with a massive window that overlooked the valley. A deck extended from either side of the grand entrance, and every inch of it screamed regal.

They entered into a massive lounge area with a grand fireplace that extended floor to beamed ceiling. Surrounding it were leather chairs and loungers, a massive stone coffee table and RJ imagined that during the winter, the fire would heat the entire building.

Balconies from rooms on the second floor overlooked the lounge, and she checked into a room next to York's and Roy's. Logan got one down the hall.

She walked into the room, and wanted to sink onto the massive bed, covered with a fur runner, and fat cotton pillows. The view looked out onto the deep-green Highcrest Mountains.

If ever they'd found a place where they might be safe, it was here.

A knock came at the door, and she opened it.

York stood in the frame. He didn't even ask—just walked in.

Just walked in, put his arm around her and pulled her to himself. Kept walking all the way until he backed her up against the wall.

"Got something on your mind there, 007?"

He grinned.

Then he kissed her. And it wasn't hard, wasn't demanding, but she'd never quite felt so engulfed, so taken by his hunger.

As if he, like she, had been thinking of his words all day.

She curled her arms around him and kissed him back, keenly, terribly aware of Angel's words. *It is my shame that I was not the one who hesitated.*

She didn't want to hesitate, either. But she knew York.

Knew his vows. And frankly, her own. So, "York," she said, pulling back. "I'm ready."

He stared at her, his chest rising and falling, those blue eyes holding hers. "RJ —"

"I'm ready to get married," she whispered.

He drew in a breath. "Okay, as soon as we get home —"

"No. Here. In Lauchtenland. Tomorrow." She pressed her hands to his chest. "I just don't want to let one more day go by without being your wife." Her gaze went to the bed, back to him.

"Oh," His eyes widened, but he smiled. "I'll make it happen."

He bent to kiss her again when a knock came at the door.

"What!" York practically roared, then turned and opened the door.

Roy stood there, his hands up. "Sorry. But we found Director Grey. And Logan needs us."

York didn't know whether to believe Landon Grey or not.

Grey was a good-looking guy with a politician haircut, white teeth and an affable smile. Late thirties, he looked and acted like a man you could trust.

No, York didn't know what to think.

They were gathered in Director Grey's suite, in the living

area with the fireplace that had probably held princes warming themselves after the hunt, or perhaps a ski.

The place was opulent—leather cigar sofas, thick green brocade draperies, a picture on the wall of some royal ancestor decked out in hunting attire, a couple dogs at his feet.

Grey sat in a cigar chair, one of his bodyguards—apparently CDC directors got bodyguards these days—standing not far away, stoic, not listening to the conversation.

Right.

He'd been a marine guard once, back in the day during his diplomatic security years. The security officer knew the full story, and York intended on grabbing him later for a shakedown. Or maybe Logan would do it, by the way he sat on the sofa, his mouth pinched.

"I had always intended on coming to Lauchtenland," Grey said. "It was in my itinerary. Right before Berlin and the international symposium on viruses."

That jived with what Logan had told them.

"So why the early exit from the conference?"

"Blame Arlo. He was leaving early and asked me to join him. We have a long-standing history of impromptu guest lectures."

Logan held up a hand. "We know you went to school with Arlo here at Haxton University."

They'd actually passed the school on the way up. Reminded York of the grandeur of Oxford's Christ Church, outside London.

Which made him think of RJ's words still lingering in his head. *"I'm ready to get married."*

RJ stood away, near the fireplace, watching him, her arms folded. He couldn't read the look on her face.

Here. In Lauchtenland. Tomorrow.

How? In between what—saving Grey's life and figuring out Martin's evil plan and getting the bounty taken off his head—

What was he thinking?

From the sofa, Logan said, "You must know about the bombing in Florence yesterday."

Grey nodded. "At the hotel..."

"In your room," Roy said. He perched on one arm of another leather cigar chair.

The color went out of Grey's face. "What?"

"The explosive was tracked to your room," said Logan.

York was watching the security agent behind Grey, and at Logan's words, his expression turned markedly concerned. He drew in a breath.

Grey turned and looked at him. "Marcus, do you know anything about this?"

Marcus was a younger man, mid-thirties, blond, wide-shouldered, a marine. He shook his head. "I'm sorry sir, no."

"What did you do with your key card when you left the hotel," Logan asked, easy, just a question.

"I still have mine," he said and then pulled it out of his jacket pocket. "I never turn them in, in case we need quick access." He handed them the card. "Why?"

"We're just trying to find out who might have had access to the room," Logan said, and it sounded like a reasonable explanation.

"Just us, and Director Grey. Even housekeeping is supervised. Duncan might know. He's in the hallway."

Duncan. Logan looked at Roy, who got up to do that very thing.

"We're still looking into the details of the bombing," Logan said, clearly leaving out the key card. He turned back to Grey. "Meanwhile, we aren't sure you're not being targeted."

"Why?"

"We don't know. But it seems as though the former CDC director's death might not have been an accident."

Director Grey swallowed. "Who would want to kill me? I'm no one."

"Clearly, you're someone," Logan said. "You have the ear of the president, if you need it, and you control the protocols for any large-scale biological attack on our country."

Grey stilled. "What do you want me to do?"

Those words York didn't expect. Maybe Logan didn't either because he looked at York.

A beat, and then Logan said, "Don't go to the ball."

"No," said RJ. She took a step toward the group. "He needs to go."

York looked at her.

"If he goes, then maybe we can figure out who is behind this."

"Surely you're not suggesting that Director Grey be bait," said Marcus. "I'm afraid we can't allow that."

Grey held up his hand. "Actually Marcus, you're not the only one who served this country in the military." He turned to York. "I'll do it."

"No," RJ said. "It doesn't have to be that dangerous. Go to the ball, yes. I know there is a VIP receiving line. And after everyone gets a good look at you in your costume, we change you out with...someone else."

And that's when she looked at York. Smiled.

A tiny chill went through him. What—?

Logan looked at him, his mouth a grim line. "You're about the same height. And you can dye your hair."

"You'll need a date, of course, and before that happens, I'll be there, watching the crowd —"

"No. No way." York turned to her. "Absolutely —"

"I'll be fine. And you'll be fine. Because Roy and Logan will be there, on overwatch."

It wasn't really a question, but she looked at Logan, as if asking.

He nodded.

"No. What if it's Martin, or Gustov after him? What if —"

"Perfect. I'll know just who to look for."

"Have you lost your mind?" He didn't mean for his voice to raise, and shoot, now he'd embarrassed her. But, "If someone is after Grey, you could get caught in the crossfire."

"They won't shoot into a crowd —"

"They just took out a *building*!"

Logan stood up. "Okay, calm down, York. No one is getting inside the building with a weapon anyway."

York cocked his head. "Please."

"We'll get the palace guard involved. They'll help us set up a perimeter. No one will be able to take a shot, or bring a weapon in."

York's mouth pinched—he could feel his entire body turning into a knot.

RJ took a step closer and softened her voice. "It's a masked ball. No one will know it's me. And, you'll be there to watch my back, too. And me, yours."

"And I'll be there," said Marcus. "I won't let anything happen to either of you."

Another beat.

"Fine. I'll talk with Roy, and we'll put a plan together," York said.

Logan turned to Director Grey. "Until then, stay here." He looked at Marcus who met his gaze with a nod.

York took RJ's hand and they walked out into the hallway.

Oh, he wanted to strangle her.

But not here, not now.

Roy stood in the hallway, talking with the other security agent, Duncan.

Same age as Marcus, dark hair, smaller build. And, he also had Marine in his countenance, his chin lifted against Roy's dark-eyed questions.

"I still have my key card," he was saying to Roy. "It's protocol to hang onto them." He reached into his jacket pocket and handed it over.

"What about the director? Did he have one?" Roy asked.

"No. It keeps him from going to the room without us. Although, I do remember him having one, now that I think about it. I took it from him when we arrived, however and gave it back to the hotel desk. Protocol."

"Who gave him the card?"

"I don't know. I think it might have been in his room when we arrived."

Logan had followed them into the hallway. "Make sure no one goes in there without being vetted," Logan said. "Even room service. Everything gets checked."

"Sir. Yes, sir."

"And no flower deliveries," said Roy.

They headed down the hall to Logan's room. Another suite, this one smaller, no fireplace, but with a sitting room, another hunting picture on the wall.

York let go of RJ's hand and stood at the door, his arms folded.

His gut still in a knot.

Logan walked over to the window, looked out at the twilight pouring over the mountain. "I believe him," He turned to look at them. "I pulled his jacket—Navy doc, served with honors before going on to get his degree in contagions. He was appointed by Jackson, but he's personal friends with White, so she might have done it to get on White's good side. He's been to White's ranch in Montana several times. And, Isaac personally vouched for him. Is even attending a worldwide security summit with him in Germany in a few weeks."

"You sure that's a good idea, boss?" Roy said.

"I need more information before I advise the president to pull out of an international summit, but no, I'm not sure."

He turned to RJ. "Are you sure this is a good idea?"

Why was he asking her? She was the first to volunteer for hazard duty. He opened his mouth to object, but she answered for him.

"Not sure, no." RJ looked at him.

Oh.

"But until we come up with something different, it's all I have." She turned to Logan. "And I trust you and Roy to figure out the best strategy."

"What about York?"

She looked at him, then headed to the door. "He has plans."

Then she winked at him and walked out.

Leaving York there to stare at Logan, nonplussed.

"Plans?"

York took a breath. "She—we—want to get married."

Roy just stared at him.

A smile tweaked Logan's face. "Finally."

York shook his head. "I dunno. An hour ago, I thought this was a brilliant idea. Now..."

"York. If you're waiting for the perfect moment, you'll wait all your life. There will always be something."

Right. Like a bounty on his head, or an international plot to destroy the world?

"Maybe I'm being morbid but what if we never get off this carousel and live a normal life."

"Maybe this is normal life, for you. But more, who says we ever get to hop off the carousel? Life keeps turning, and sure, you might take a break, but the fact is, when we're in the employ of the Lord, we get back on, keep fighting the good fight. And not everyone's fight looks like ours, no, but the journey is a struggle for everyone. Life is not meant to be easy. It's meant to be something that makes us cling to God." He put a hand on York's shoulder. "Go, get married. Roy and I got this."

York considered him. "Nothing can happen to her. Nothing. Swear it."

Logan gave him a look.

"I swear," Roy said.

He let out a breath. "Okay. But can we even get married here? Don't I need a license?"

"Yes, you do," Roy said. "But Lauchtenland is like Gretna Green, in Scotland. It's a marriage getaway. People from around the world come here to elope."

York would love to know how Roy knew that.

"Are you sure you shouldn't invite the family?" Logan said. "I've met her brothers. Well, at least Ford, and Tate, and —"

"This is what she wants," York said. "And you know the Marshalls. They show up and suddenly there's drama."

"More than explosions and kidnappings and assassinations?"

Point, Logan.

He smiled. "Okay. I'll see if we can rustle you up a preacher."

"And a church, if you would." York headed to the door.

Roy followed him out into the hallway. "You're sure about this?"

York turned. Paused.

"In my bones, I know RJ and I are meant to be together. And ever since the bombing yesterday, I can't help but feel like if we don't do this now, then..." He sighed. "Something's coming, Roy. Maybe I'm just feeling a shadow over my shoulder with this bounty on my head. Or maybe it's just that sense you get when you know someone's following you, right?"

Roy nodded slowly.

"But I can't help but believe this is it. I need to marry RJ now. Because Logan is right. We don't know what tomorrow will bring and I...I don't want to wait another day. Not another minute."

A beat, then, "Okay, then we have no choice."

York frowned.

"It's time for the bachelor party." Roy grinned and threw his arm over York's shoulder. "I feel like it's time for you to meet my old mate, Gunner Ferguson, protection officer to the future king. He'll know just where to spend your last night of freedom."

CHAPTER NINE

Their story just had to end happily. Because RJ simply refused to believe anything else.

"Coffee, miss?"

She sat on the outside deck of the Royal Lodge, overlooking the grandeur of Hadsby Castle, the hamlet of Dunholm.

"Yes, please."

The castle was straight out of a fairytale, a motte and bailey construction, with the keep on a rise, a walled courtyard or bailey, surrounded by a palisade and what was once a moat, perhaps, but was now a flower garden.

One side of the palisade led to woods and the mew, or stables.

Another side, the entrance, was gated, and guarded, like Windsor Castle, with the gate opening to a cobblestone drive that led to Old Dunholm.

Four drum towers anchored the corners of the castle, topped with parapets. The flag of Lauchtenland flapped from the western rampart.

Yes, she'd entered a fairytale, because today, she was getting married.

York had left a note, wrapped inside was his credit card under her door.

Buy a dress.

Sweet. And maybe he meant for a ball, but given his reaction to her idea last night, probably not.

If he could, he'd put her in one of those towers like a medieval king, just to keep her safe.

Frankly, she might do the same to him, if she were queen of the land.

But it was a good plan, if they wanted to both keep Director Grey safe and find out who might be trying to kill him.

Chances were that no one would make an attempt on his life during a royal ball, anyway. And then she'd have a night of dancing with her own personal prince.

She was downright brilliant, if she had to say so herself.

The waiter returned with fresh coffee and set a croissant and scrambled eggs in front of her. "Anything else, ma'am?"

She looked at him. Nice looking young man, lean, he wore a black apron, black pants and a white oxford with RL emblazoned on the breast pocket.

"Do you know where I might find a wedding dress around here?"

"Oh, there are many such shops, especially in new Dunholm."

"What about in old town? Any vintage shops there?"

"There is one. Simply called Shop Vintage. It has everything, and a few years ago, Princess Daffy found her blue ball gown there. It's on main street, in the hamlet."

"Perfect. Thank you." She turned to her eggs and opened the book.

When she'd finished reading last night, Angelica was in

real trouble. The SS had rounded up partigianos in Lucca and was questioning—and executing them—one by one. She'd sneaked into town to see if her brother was among the captured, but didn't see him.

But her questions had raised the attention of the Obergruppenfüehrer, who saw her in town.

And had followed her back to the house to confront her.

Chapter 18/Portami a casa: un ricordo della resistenza italiana

Of course I am afraid of him. He is a big man, tall, with a presence that raises the skin on my neck, turns my stomach. Thus far, he has left me alone to cook, clean after him, but I know better.

He watches me.

Probably, waiting for a reason to force me into something tawdry.

It's been nearly a month since Fred has left me. I now know the truth. Despite my prayers, he will not return. Of course not. It is too dangerous.

He has his duty. His life. And I have mine.

It was a foolish dream.

One that feels even more simpleminded when the Obergruppenfüehrer darkens my kitchen door.

I am kneading dough, my hands floured and thus I am helpless when he walks over to me and grabs my wrists. He speaks in German, of course, but I feel that he must see right through me, read my eyes because he looks at me with such suspicion.

"You are looking for your brother."

His words are in English, and they jolt me. So much that I yank my arm back, breathing hard.

"He is with the resistance?"

I freeze because a faint hope whistles through me. What if he doesn't know? I could...I—

And then he laughs. It is sharp, and deep and cruel.

I can't move.

Even when he takes two steps toward me, grabs my face with a strong hand and pushes me against the wall. "I will find him. And I will kill him."

My breath is faint within me. Then he steps back and his gaze scans over me. I feel undressed, naked, abused.

"Or I could forget about. He could be nothing." He lifts his shoulder. Then he sticks his finger in the tomato sauce I've made for the calzones. Licks it off. "Delicious."

I will throw the batch out. Then I will run. In my heart, I know Tory is gone, and here, I have nothing.

I will run to the border, through the Gothic line and find Fred.

It is better than living with this—

The Obergruppenfüehrer steps close again, runs the back of his fingers down my face. "You are so beautiful."

I didn't see him enter, and thank St. Anthony, the patron saint of miracles because just like that, the Obergruppenfüehrer drops.

The cast iron skillet that hit him is held by...

Fred.

He stands in the shadows, whole, real and very angry, the gold of his eyes in mine.

I launch myself at him, my arms around his neck, and he sweeps me up, drags me away from the brute on the floor, bleeding from the head.

Fred carries me out the kitchen door, into the sunlight, where I see him clearly, see the worry in his eyes. "You're here."

He brushes the hair from my face with his strong hands. "Of course I am here. You are my heart, Angel. My heart, my life, belongs to you."

Then he kisses me. His touch envelopes me even as he closes me in his arms. He is strength and hope and in it I know that I am safe, so I kiss him back, giving myself over to him.

He shouldn't be here. I know this. This is a terrible mistake for him to come back to me—but while my head knows this, my heart clings to him.

He finally raises his head, breathing hard. "Do you trust me?"

Is the sky blue, the vineyard full of grapes, the sun risen?

He takes my hand. "It's not far, but we must go now."

I have no idea where we are going, but he takes me through the grotto, to the far side where the trail leads to a valley, then...

"No, Fred—it is too dangerous." I pull back because—

"They will harbor us," he says, drawing me close, his hands on my arms. "It is a place of God. It is safe there."

I want to believe him. The Carthusian monastery has remained untouched for now, but...

"We can be married."

Oh. I meet his eyes. They are glossy. "Will you marry me?"

Yes. I throw my arms around him, and we are lost in a long moment of hope.

Then we run with our whole hearts to the monastery. He must have arranged our arrival because they open the gates for us and Father Cantero takes us in.

"Thank you, Father," I say to him. He wears the simple robes of a monk, bald head, kind smile as he brings us in.

"If it were Jesus knocking at the door, would I refuse him entry?" He looks at Fred, and I am suddenly reminded of his race. But it seems the monks, like me, care only for his heart, his bravery.

And Father Cantero seems to know why we are there. He leads us to a chamber, a prayer room and lights a candle.

Now?

Fred takes my hands. "We met on the road. He is also with the underground."

A tremble shakes through me. "I know this. They hide Jews —"

"And others, perhaps. But tonight, they also hide us."

I am ready and I turn to Father Cantero who is pronouncing wedding rites over us. I am not certain this is legal, but it is a wedding, nonetheless, before God. There is no one to ask questions, just Fred and I to give our assent, then he blesses us and Fred produces a ring.

"Where did you get this?"

"A shop in Pisa." It is just a simple gold band, twisted with three cords.

He makes his promise, and marries me. And I make mine.

Father Cantero blesses us, and we are wed.

I am sure the private chambers charterhouse have never been used for the wedding night, but Father Cantero says nothing as he leads us to a second story room.

It overlooks the courtyard, a wide arched window in the stone walls, a red terrazzo floor and in the center of the room, a narrow bed.

"We will bring up something to eat," he says. "Later." Then he smiles as he leaves the room, and we must be indeed blessed to find ourselves at this moment.

Miracles.

The afternoon sunlight washes the room in shades of orange and gold as Fred turns to me.

I am suddenly shy, all of it cascading over me. Tory, the attack of the Oppenheimer, and now—

"Shh," he says, and pulls me against him. "We have no hurry. Not yet." He kisses my forehead, then pulls me down to sit on the bed next to him and wraps his arms around me. "Now, you will forever be my home."

No hurry. I breathe out the words. Yes. "And you will forever be my home."

I kiss him. And he kisses me, gently. Perfectly.

Then he lays me back on the bed and we know each other,

finally.

RJ stuck the bookmark into the folds of the pages and closed the book.

See, if Angel and Fred, in the middle of war, could find a moment of peace, of joy, then she and York could, too.

So, maybe this wasn't a crazy idea, after all.

Her mother even agreed. She'd called her early this morning, after ten p.m. Montana time, but her mother was still up. And waiting for the news of her engagement, apparently, because York had of course asked her mother for her blessing.

Thinking of everything, even if this did feel rushed.

"Of course I'd like to be there for your wedding day, but you need to marry York, anywhere, anytime. The poor man has waited long enough. We'll celebrate when you get home."

"I'm not sure he was serious. But if he is—"

"Marry the man, RJ. With my blessing. I just don't want to be the one to tell your brothers." She'd laughed.

No kidding. But someday they'd have to figure out that she could take care of herself. "Thanks, Mom. I love you."

Now, RJ signed her bill to her room, left a tip, then headed out to the guest area. Funny she hadn't seen York at all. What if he'd changed...

"Miss Marshall, you have a message."

The concierge, a man dressed in a green velvet suitcoat, gloves, black pants came around the desk near the door. He handed her an envelope.

She opened it and pulled out a note.

York's handwriting. Choppy, bold strokes, all caps.

King Rein's Chapel, 3pm.

What?

She looked at the man. "When was this delivered?"

"Approximately two hours ago, ma'am, on the gentleman's way in."

York had been out before six a.m.?

Or rather, maybe he'd been just coming back in?

She pocketed the note. "I'm headed to old Dunholm."

"Take the cobblestone drive, ma'am. It will lead you right down Centre Street."

She headed down the street, looking for Shop Vintage. She didn't need anything fancy, just something suitable.

After all, Angel got married in a day frock dusted with flour.

She found the storefront halfway down Centre Street. A bell attached to a red ribbon jangled as she opened the door.

Time was stored here, in the antique knickknacks, books and China doll sets. Tables filled with bolts of cloth, pictures and toys from ages past filled the center tables.

The place smelled of age, of life lived and savored.

Along the wall hung racks of dresses, shirt and slacks.

She picked up an off white, knee length dress in satin, lace around the bodice. It would do. But it didn't...dazzle her.

Oh, she was being silly. What did she expect—to turn into a princess?

She found another—this one a light pink garden dress with puffy sleeves. She could go as Anne of Green Gables.

She put the dresses back. Sighed.

"May I help you?"

A woman had come out of the back. Tiny, round face, kind eyes, white-brillo pad hair.

RJ sighed. "I don't know. I'm looking for a gown."

"For the upcoming Rosendans?"

"Actually, for...I'm getting married this afternoon."

To say the words aloud sent a chill through her. "What —"

"Oh. A bride." The woman came up to her. "Then you need a dress from the back."

She led RJ around the corner to a smaller alcove. The back appeared to be living quarters, through a narrow door. Here, in the antechamber, a number of party masks, with feathers and sequins lay on an ancient table, a standing mirror in the middle. Other baubles—necklaces, bracelets, rings—spilled out of containers onto the table.

But on a rack against the wall hung a handful of off-white gowns. “Donated by our local brides over the years.”

The front bell jangled, and the storekeeper left to greet her new customer.

RJ looked through them. Pretty enough—some satin with plunging necklines—she wasn’t sure she could pull that off. One with a simple bodice, a chiffon skirt. A mermaid dress in sequins.

None that felt like...her.

She stood in front of a gilded oval mirror, trying to decide what was...her. Her dark hair was down, her face plain—all her makeup had burned in the fire. She wore a pair of jeans, runners and tee-shirt.

She could probably get married in a burlap sack for all the flair she had.

“Did you try the box?” said a voice.

She turned and followed the shopkeeper’s gesture to a blue box on the floor. “You never know what you’ll find until you open the box.”

Funny. But RJ leaned down and lifted the cover.

Oh. My. Inside lay a pale gold tulle evening gown. Sleeveless, with straps covered with pink and gold sequins.

She pulled it out. The bodice was heavily embellished with shimmering pink and purple sequins amidst swirling vines of metallic copper gilt threadwork that ran vertically down the bodice to a wide waist panel and flowing floor length skirt. The skirt itself was made of two layers of tulle over a peach underskirt.

Clusters of frosted white pearls and beads accented the sweetheart neckline.

"It looks like you have found a dress by Taffron Bjork."

"Who?"

The woman came up to her. "Taffron was a dress designer whose gowns were worn by royalty. Specifically, three of our princesses. Princess Louisa, Princess Catherine, who is our current Queen, and Princess Daffy, Prince Gus's wife. He died years ago, but the rumor has it that he made numerous other gowns which were never found." She touched the dress almost reverently. "It is said that his dresses were designed by God, to be worn only for the right woman, someone who would be blessed with something magical."

She met RJ's eyes. "Clearly, this dress is meant for you."

Oh. She opened her mouth. Closed it. "Let's see if it fits."

"It will fit." But the woman stepped away and pointed to a small room, covered with a curtain.

Please let her not destroy the dress. RJ stepped into the room, pulled off her clothing, took the straps of her bra down and then pulled on the dress.

Glory be, it fit.

As if, indeed, the dress had been made for her. It slid down her body, accentuated her waist, and hello, she even had cleavage, although admittedly, not much.

But perfect for this dress.

It fell to her ankles, the hem scalloped and also beaded.

She practically shimmered, even in the dim light of the fitting room.

Throwing open the curtain, she stepped out for better lighting and a view in the full length, gilded mirror.

"Wow."

The word came from a young woman trying on masks at the table. Light-brown skin, black corkscrew hair, hazel-green eyes, she looked about eighteen in her skinny jeans, flip-flops and floral shirt. She set down a black feathered mask. "Is that for the Rosendans?"

"Um...maybe." RJ turned and swept her gaze over herself in the mirror. Maybe the dress was too glitzy, too elegant. "I'm getting married in about five hours, so...I was thinking—"

"Yes. A thousand times, yes." The woman stepped up to her. "It's unique and gorgeous and perfect. And, if you want to wear it to the ball, too, it might go amazing with this."

She handed her a gold rhinestone mask with florets and swirls and a tall peacock feather. RJ put it to her face and couldn't help but laugh. "This is crazy."

"Who is doing your hair and makeup?"

"Oh, um—I...I hadn't—"

"We'll use my mom's stylist. She's amazing." She grabbed her phone and started to text. Then looked up at RJ. "Take the dress off. We need to get you shoes, and a bra and..." She looked her over. "We have serious work to do."

RJ just stared at her.

"My name is Imani, by the way. Nice to meet you. Now, hurry up."

Ten minutes later, RJ had checked out with the dress, the mask, a vintage 1930's art deco necklace with three teardrop crystals and matching earrings.

And shoes. Gold lace wedding heels, like she might be Cinderella or something.

She sort of felt like it. Especially when she and Imani exited the shop and she followed Imani back up the cobblestone street toward the palace.

"Does your mom work at the palace?" She asked as the front gate of Hadsby Castle opened for the girl.

Imani smiled. "Sort of."

"Your accent—it sounds midwestern. Or southern. Are you American?"

"Born in Hearts Bend, Tennessee," she said, then greeted a woman dressed in palace household staff attire, blue dress, emblem on the breast. "Hello Maggie. We're going to use the Princess Charlotte guest suite."

Maggie nodded to her. "Very good, ma'am."

Oh. So not staff.

Imani led her through a grand gallery, through an old, massive library and down a hallway until she reached a door.

It opened to a small apartment, and they walked into a sitting room. The grand window overlooked the grounds to the north, a lush lawn and tended garden, overflowing with roses of all color. Beyond that, far below the high cliffs and beyond, the sea churned a deep blue.

A woman in her early forties, perhaps with auburn hair and deep-green eyes, wearing an apron, had set up shop in the room, covering the flooring and one of the blue velvet chairs with a drape. She curtsied. "Your highness. Ma'am."

Your *highness?*

She looked at Imani.

"My mother is Princess Gemma," she said with a smile.

"Princess Gemma, married to Crown Prince John?"

"That's the one. And this is her stylist, Eloise."

"Please sit, ma'am." Eloise gestured to the chair and RJ had nothing but to sit.

How...?

"Oh, you have wonderful hair. What shall we do with it?" Eloise held out a hand mirror to her.

"Um. Nothing fancy —"

"Nope. It'll be fancy. She's getting married in..." Imani glanced at the clock. "Four hours!"

"Shush!" Eloise stepped back. "Well then, we must to work."

Three hours later, RJ didn't recognize herself. Eloise had washed, conditioned, waxed and coiffed her dark hair into a bouffant chignon. From her face, her hair fell away in a soft wave, gathered up behind her head where more curls and waves folded over each other into a gentle perfect next of glamour.

"Now all we need is a tiara."

RJ had spent the time getting to know Imani, who told her a story of tragedy that could break anyone's heart.

"My mother and father fell in love in high school, married, had me, and then my mother just dropped dead from an aneurysm. My dad died of a broken heart, although he really just fell asleep at the wheel in a one car accident. My grandfather died, then and my grandmother was too broken to take me, so Gemma took me in. She was sort of a rescuer of all things, including, I think Prince John."

"I read about his wife, Holland's tragic death, years ago."

"Yes, terrible. And she was expecting. He came over to Hearts Bend for personal reasons but met Gemma there and fell in love. It took a little doing, but she finally agreed to marry him. And then they adopted me."

"Your mom sounds amazing."

"She is. But more, God is. He did this. We had nothing. Death. Destruction. Humiliation. Now we have new clothes, new titles. We are royalty." Imani had picked out makeup, too, and after Eloise finished her hair, she went to work on her face. RJ stopped her at the false lashes, but agreed to the gold eye shadow, the red lips the mascara.

The woman who stared back at her in the mirror was every inch a princess.

She had no idea where RJ had vanished to.

Oh boy.

"Beautiful."

The voice came from the door, and Eloise turned. "Your royal highness." She curtsied, as did Imani, and RJ just sat there, not sure what to do.

"Um," she made to gather the makeup brushes left in her lap.

"Stay seated. I'm still not used to it." The woman came into the room. Tall and regal, she wore her deep-chestnut-brown hair back and up, in a similar, if not as fancy chignon, a pair of dress pants and a floral blouse. Her blue eyes settled on RJ, kind. "I needed to meet this American Imani has been texting me about."

She came over. "Just call me Gemma. We Americans have to stick together." Gemma gave a glance to Eloise, then her work. "Breathtaking."

"I really don't recognize myself," RJ said.

"Most brides don't. They're dazzled by what they see in the groom's eyes. And that's exactly how it should be. Love should transform us, make us realize that we are set apart." She leaned in. "That each of us are princesses."

RJ laughed. "I'm a cowgirl, not a princess."

"Tell that to your groom," Gemma said. She winked. "Imani says you'll be attending the Rosendans."

"Yes."

"Lovely. Well, I won't tell a soul that I have seen this dress before." She picked it up from the blue box. "Enchanting." She held it out to RJ. "Let's get you dressed."

It took the crowd, it seemed, to slide the dress over her head without upsetting her hair and makeup, but twenty minutes later, she stood, fully dressed, her feet in the golden heels, resplendent in a full-length mirror that Princess Gemma had brought in.

"Your groom is a lucky man."

"Oh, I think it's me who is lucky," RJ said.

"You need these." Imani handed her a pair of white, elbow length gloves.

"And this." Gemma gestured to a butler, standing near the door. He came in holding a box. Gemma opened it.

"Oh, no I can't—"

"Calm down. The baubles aren't real diamonds. It's one of our fakes, that we use for our costumes. It was on display here a few years ago when Daffy, our then curator, created a vintage wedding dress display. This was on the Princess Louisa's display."

She put the simple tiara on her head. The pearl-encrusted crown sat perfectly on her head, the diamond-like chips glittering in the light.

"Are you sure?"

"You can wear it to the ball and return it then." Gemma leaned down. "Happy wedding day."

"She needs to get to the church." Imani stood behind her.

RJ glanced at the wall clock. "I'm late. Already—oh York will think I'm not coming."

"You'll be fine. If he loves you, he'll wait. We'll get you there." Imani held a bag with her clothing in it. "I'll have this delivered to the Royal Lodge. You, come with me."

She followed Imani and Gemma to the front walk.

A shiny Rolls Royce stood in the cobbled driveway, a footman at the open door. "Seriously?"

"Why not?" Gemma said. "Thank you for allowing us to share in your beautiful day."

RJ curtsied, and Gemma laughed. "Okay then."

The footman helped RJ in, and she settled back in the plush red velvet as the driver left the courtyard. She lifted a gloved hand like she might actually be royal and waved to her attendants.

Okay, this felt crazy. But perfect, maybe. And she couldn't wait to see York's face.

God did this.

So maybe she should stop being so afraid that she had to do something amazing with her life. Maybe she could just step back, let God take over.

"King Rein's Chapel was built just opposite the portico that used to stand as a forward fortification of defense to the castle." Her driver was an elderly man and now he pointed to a flat area. "Now the queen likes to take tea there and survey the kingdom."

Indeed.

"The king's men used to use the chapel for prayer before they left for battle."

He drove up to a small stone building with an arched door and a steepled entrance. Yellow and white climbing roses framed the wooden door, which hung open.

The driver helped her out, giving her his hand. "Such a shame you have no one to walk you down the aisle, miss."

"Oh. My father is with me," she said.

"Still." He walked over, and pulled off a singular white rose, brought it back for her. Bowed. "He would tell you that you look exquisite, ma'am."

He handed her the rose.

"Thank you." She waited until he drove away.

Drew in her breath.

Then, she entered the doorway. Arched windows on either side let in light, the stone white, just a few hand-hewn benches with polished wood on either side of the aisle. Lit candles flickered from two hanging chandeliers. The place smelled of legacy and hope.

She stepped inside the chamber. A spray of fresh flowers sat on an altar in the front.

Beside that stood a man. He seemed old, but sturdy, and was dressed in a simple pair of pants, a clean shirt, open at the neck. He looked up at her. Blue eyes, maybe, but they settled on her, and something brushed through her.

Oh no.

He gave her a tight smile.

And that's when she realized.

York wasn't here.

She stood at the top of the aisle, holding her flower, in her golden dress and something dropped out of her. Hope, maybe.

"He's not here."

The man took a breath. "No. He was here. But, I'm afraid he left, ma'am."

York loved it when a plan came together.

He'd put together impulsive, high-risk missions before, but none felt as cobbled together, and fraught with danger as his impromptu, had-to-be-perfect wedding to RJ.

And yet, he'd done it.

Roy was right to call Gunner Ferguson. The chap had picked them up at the Royal Lodge and brought them right to the Belly of the Beast, where the planning had commenced.

Apparently, Roy and Gunner had run some training ops together while they both served in special forces. He liked Gunner. Quiet, serious, he wore his dark hair shaved short, bore his weight in his shoulders and torso, and stared through a man with his deep-set, blue eyes until he finally broke into a smile.

Held out his hand. “Any friend of Roy’s is a mate of mine.”

Gunner ordered them a couple deep-brown lagers from Ernst, the barkeep.

Ernst delivered them to their table, with a “Food?”

Gunner ordered a couple baskets of chips then got down to business.

Licenses—no problem. He knew a guy at the clerk’s office who could get it done.

Location—King Rein’s chapel, built in 1066, on one of the pinnacles that overlooked the hamlet of Dunholm. He even knew a minister and pulled up his phone.

While Ernst delivered the frothy beer, he’d nailed down a suit for York from Crown Prince John’s own tailor and managed to procure an appointment with the royal jeweler.

Ernst delivered the chips right about the time the minister called back and said he was out of town.

But Ernst, man of exactly the right, if not few words, said, cryptically, “Emmanuel. Best preacher. Love marriage.”

Whatever that meant, but Gunner gave a grunt of approval, nodded, and sent the man away.

Then, they moved on to the honeymoon.

“You can’t stay at the Royal Lodge,” he said. “I’ll talk to Prince John and see if you can stay in the turret at Hadsby Castle. Prince Gus just finished remodeling it.”

York blinked at him. “The...castle?”

Gunner had laughed, put his hand on his shoulder. “They have eighty rooms, York. Most of them empty. The turret overlooks the sea—it’s breathtaking. If I ever got married, I’d take my bride there.”

He picked up his phone again to text.

York couldn’t imagine it—having a direct line to the crown prince.

"I'm texting Shaw, Prince John's personal attendant, to confirm."

York ate one of the chips—aka, waffle fries—and downed it with the salty beer as Roy turned to the matter of the CDC director and a rundown of everything they knew—and wanted to find out.

Gunner listened, his mouth a grim line as Roy also detailed the last two weeks, starting with the moment Alan Martin had shown up outside a Paris coffeehouse, to stopping a EMP bomb attack in Italy, to the kidnapping and liberation in Germany of an orphan Russian girl, the near assassination attempt, and finally the bombing in Florence.

The protection officer leaned back, his back to the wall, arms folded over his chest. "I don't like you bringing trouble to Lauchtenland, Roy."

"Not us who brought trouble, mate."

Gunner nodded. "Fair enough."

"And we'll do our best to keep it away from you. But we can't whisk Director Grey out of the country without arousing or garnering attention, especially if we want to figure out what is going on."

"I just don't want trouble at the Rosendans. The Queen is not in the best of health, and this may be her last Garden event. It must go well."

York understood the desire to protect their royals. As far as he could understand, Lauchtenland ran much like England, with the sovereign more of a figurehead than a true ruler, but they still held the country together.

"We'll be watching the dance, and York will pose as the CDC director after the dance starts. If they try anything, we'll catch them."

Gunner drew in a breath, nodded. "I'll get in contact with the Captain of the Palace Guard, and we'll post extra guards, as well as watch your man." He took a drink of his beer. "And you and your bride, York."

"Thanks, Gunner."

From behind them, the door opened to a starry night, and a man walked in. He wore a woolen anorak and wide brimmed hat, leather boots.

A coat, in the middle of summer?

"Emmanuel." The name summoned from Ernst, and he nodded at the table. "There. See. Marriage.

"That's why I'm here." The man came over. He wore a hint of a beard, longer brown hair, and had a kindness about his eyes that settled through York. "Who is getting married?

"Me." York said.

Emmanuel scooted onto the bench beside Roy, his work worn hands on the table. He ran his palm across it, as if assessing the table.

"Are you a preacher?"

"Sometimes."

"Can you marry us."

"Marriage is a divine union. Are you ready?"

York looked at him. "I love her more than life itself. She is my home. She is my always."

Emmanuel smiled. "Then, yes." He stood up. "At King Rein's Chapel, three p.m."

"Sounds good." York held out his hand. The preacher took it. Warm. Solid. And then he smiled.

"I'm glad to see you here, York Newgate."

York had nothing, even as Emmanuel left. Then he sank down onto the bench. "I don't remember giving him my name."

Gunner grinned. "It's Emmanuel. He knows your name, York."

Huh?

But Gunner's phone buzzed, and it was Prince Gus himself, agreeing to give York the turret suite.

"And he says to stop by the garden in the morning, early, and he will show you the secret entrance."

How-*dy*.

They spent way too long, then, sharing stories, playing darts and by the time they left, laughing as they walked back to the hotel, the night late and arching over them, York had added Gunner to his list of true mates.

He felt like a king, really, especially when York rose early, went to the castle—yes, castle—and was let in the gate by the morning guard.

He made his way to the garden and nearly fell over when Prince Gus himself met him. He knew the man from the tabloids, years ago, but wasn't prepared for the solemn royal he met dressed in riding clothes. He had dark hair, the blue eyes of his namesake and held out his hand to York.

York didn't know if he was supposed to bow or—he lowered his head. "Your...Highness."

"Gus is fine. Do you play polo?"

"No, sorry," York said.

He sighed. "I prefer rugby, but the Queen hates blood. Come with me, I'll show you the turret."

He walked through the garden toward the grass, edging toward the building. "My guess is that you won't want to come in through the main gate." He turned and pointed toward the woods. "There is a side gate. I'll give you the combination, but it leads right from King Rein's Chapel, through the woods, to here." Then he pressed away a tangle of vines and revealed a door. "I don't use it often, but when I was young, my brother John and I used to sneak out of the castle." He winked.

Then he opened the door to a narrow, stone staircase that

spiraled up. It was held together by rugged beams. York stuck his head in. "Where does it go?"

"Up."

York looked at him. Gus laughed. "Take it up, all the way. You'll come out in the royal wing. Don't worry, it's secured, so you can't get in, but from there, go down the hallway, and you'll come to another door. That leads to the turret."

"Thank you, Gus," he said. "I don't know what to say."

"If I can't share the beauty of this world, then what good is it? By the way, stop by the garden and pick up some flowers for the church altar on your way out. Happy nuptials."

Indeed.

He retrieved the flowers, then headed back to the hotel to put them in water, and left a note for RJ at the concierge.

Next he ventured into town to buy a ring.

Five hours later, he stood outside King Rein's Chapel, swept up by the fragrance of the arching roses, his heart thudding in his chest.

Sheesh, he hadn't felt this nervous since...well, maybe since the day he'd married Claire. He'd told himself, after Claire's death, that he'd never marry again. But this was different. He was older, wiser, and RJ wasn't Claire.

And frankly, he missed the commitment of marriage. The power of it to strengthen him, give him purpose. Bind him to the man he longed to be.

Footsteps fell on the gravel behind him, and Emmanuel walked up. He had changed clothes, wore a simple white shirt, a pair of pants, those boots. And his over-sized hat. But he carried a bible and came up to York with an outstretched hand.

"Waiting for the bride?"

York nodded.

"I know what that feels like." He went inside the chapel.

York checked his watch. She still had a few minutes.

Admittedly, he had knocked on her door a couple hours ago, breaking the no-see-the-bride tradition.

She wasn't there.

He refused to panic. Then.

Now.

He'd go inside and wait with Emmanuel.

The stone room smelled of the fresh bouquet of flowers that he'd brought from the castle garden.

Emmanuel stood silently with him as York stood at the altar.

And waited.

And waited.

He could taste his pulse even as he looked again at his watch. Ten minutes late.

She was coming. She was—

A figure shadowed the doorway of the chapel, moving into the foyer. He glanced at Emmanuel and grinned.

Turned back.

Oh. Ziggy stood in the doorway, looking travel weary and stressed. He braced himself for—well, *something*—as she strode down the altar toward him.

"Roy said you'd be here."

Um, yes. "I'm getting married."

"Well, duh. But first, you have to know something." She hooked him by the arm, glanced at Emmanuel, frowned, then dragged York out the side door.

Roy stood there, hand on his hip, pacing.

"What is this—an intervention?"

"Gregori is dead."

York stared at Ziggy.

"Yeah. Really dead. As in his wife and granddaughter were killed too."

York pressed his hand to his mouth, feeling sick. He turned.

"They were killed a few hours after you met with him, in Berlin."

Roy must have already known this because he shook his head. "Gregori must have given us away, but maybe not for gain."

"Or his hired killer turned on him." Ziggy said.

"Was there anything—"

"Yeah. This was carved into his chest." She held up her phone.

It showed a snap of a man's chest, with a jagged circle, a star in the middle.

"A roundstone."

"Yes." She pocketed the phone. "You know what this means."

He wanted to turn and punch something.

"York?"

He stilled and now he did turn.

Oh. RJ stood in front of him, and he just. Couldn't. Breathe.

She was dressed in a gold dress that practically glittered, her dark hair up in some sort of regal twist, her eyes impossibly blue and wearing a crown on her head.

Like she might be marrying a prince.

He looked at her and pressed his hand to his mouth.

"Are you okay?" She stepped out from the chapel, put her hand on his arm.

He shook his head. "I..."

"He'll be okay," Roy said and clamped a hand on him. "You go inside with Ziggy. He'll be there in a minute."

"No. No more secrets." She looked at Ziggy. "What did you find out on your top-secret mission that isn't top secret, York."

He stared at her. *What?*

"We don't know who put the hit out on York, but it's being fulfilled by a group called the Orphans. It's a..."

"It's a murder squad," Roy said. "Lethal, and unrelenting."

York looked at her. "RJ —"

"Okay. Everybody inside." She looked at York. "We're having words."

Roy looked at Ziggy, then shrugged.

She walked up to him. "I'm wearing heels. And a gold dress. And makeup."

"You look..."

"I'm freakin' breathtaking."

He stared at her, and something in his chest just...released. "Yes, yes you are."

"So what, what are you going to do about it?"

He blinked at her.

"We're not going backwards, York. We've come so far—and enough with the secrets. I know about the bounty. I know there's trouble. But I was standing in there, talking to Emmanuel, thinking you'd left me, and you know what he did?"

"Told you that probably you shouldn't marry me?"

"Please. He read the psalms. Aloud. The Lord is near to all who call upon them. He will fulfill the desires of those who fear him. He will also hear their cry and will save them." She put her hand on his chest. "The Lord keeps all those who love him."

He swallowed.

"York. This entire time, we forgot that God is with us. He has not abandoned us. And he won't abandon us. I know God will fight for us, even if we don't ask him, but how much more will he come to our aid when we are kneeled, together, as one, depending on him?"

She touched his face. "A cord of three strands can't be broken. So get in this chapel and marry me so we can join forces and fight this, with God."

He breathed in her words, let them settle into his bones.

Join forces. Fight this, with God.

Her gaze burned into him. "Did I mention I'm wearing a tiara?"

He smiled. Touched her forehead with his. "You do look stunning."

"Of course I do." She took his hand. "Now, let's take this again, from the top. I'll meet you at the altar."

She kissed his cheek and walked around the building to the front.

Right. He went back inside through the back door.

Roy sat on a bench on the groom's side, beside Ziggy.

He found his place beside Emmanuel, crossed his hands.

"She is worth the wait," Emmanuel said.

York glanced at him, and the man winked.

And then York's bride came down the aisle. The afternoon sun fell through the windows, gilding the stone floor, and she walked through puddles of gold, her dress shimmering in the light.

Her gaze, however, had pinned him and he couldn't move.

He will fulfill the desires of those who fear him.

Oh, God, help me trust you.

He reached out his hand, and RJ took it as she reached the altar. Then Emmanuel stepped up and prayed.

York couldn't remember exactly what he said, but somehow, during the breadth of it, his heart had settled, his body relaxed. And when he lifted his head...

He was back in the game.

Yes, I do, and forever and Amen and he put a wedding band on RJ's finger that he'd purchased out of the vintage section, that had come from some royal collection. Hand engraved, white gold, with tiny diamonds along the band. It butted up perfectly with her engagement ring.

"Kiss your bride," Emmanuel said quietly.

York could have lost himself in her kiss, but he kept it chaste, if not lingering.

Then Emmanuel pronounced them man and wife.

He didn't remember much after that—thanking Emmanuel, promising to meet Roy and Ziggy tomorrow—until he'd climbed the stone steps through the private passageway to the royal hall, and then to the turret.

"Are you serious?" RJ said as she walked inside.

The place was opulent—stone floors cast with lush pile rugs, a velvet blue sofa faced a massive king-sized bed with a draped crown headboard. A spray of white roses sat in a vase on a tall milk-white dresser.

RJ walked to the window. "I can see all the garden from here—and even the lawn beyond to the cliffs. And maybe the shores of Germany. Or that could be Denmark."

Thank you, Prince Gus. York knew he—or maybe his wife, Princess Daffy—was behind the fresh flowers, the bottle of champagne, the tray of tapas—crostini, chocolates, soft cheeses, shrimp in a bowl of ice.

The bed had been piled with fresh white pillows and a fluffy comforter.

York walked over to RJ and stood behind her at the window, putting his hand on her waist. "Mrs. Newgate. You're the only view I care about."

She turned in his arms, put hers over his shoulders. "You all right?"

He nodded. "Now I am." He bent and kissed her and put in much more of what he'd wanted to convey at the wedding chapel.

He didn't have to hold back, didn't have to bank his touch with the ever present—*wait.*

Even still, he stepped back, gave her room.

She'd never been married, like him. Never...

He took a breath. "Do you want something to eat?"

"I'm not hungry." She took a step toward him. Touched his chest. "Are you?"

He caught her hand, brought it to his mouth. Kissed it. "Nope."

"York, you look nervous."

He drew in a breath.

"Listen, 007. I promise to take good care of you. Nothing will happen to you on my watch." Then she reached behind her and pulled the zipper of her dress. "You're safe with me."

Hardly.

But maybe...yes. Because this was marriage.

Commitment. Belief.

Trust.

Her dress fell in a soft rustle into a golden puddle on the floor.

Oh. His breath caught.

She stepped out of her shoes. "Are you ready?"

His voice fell as his gaze savored the view. "I've never been more ready for anything in my life."

Then she closed the gap, put her arms around him, and kissed him. Her touch was soft as the twilight settled into the room, the colors of rose gold and lavender. And, as he lowered them onto the bed and ran his hand down her body, familiarizing himself with his wife, knowing her, letting her know him, the truth sank deep into his core.

He was finally home.

CHAPTER
TEN

"I don't want the fairytale to end." RJ sat at the round table in the turret, eating a breakfast of strawberries and creme over thick waffles delivered to their door under plate hoods, with steaming dark coffee and spicy breakfast sausages. "I still can't quite figure out how this happened."

York sat across from her, dressed in a linen shirt, jeans and slip-on shoes he'd picked up in the hamlet yesterday as they'd wandered around on their "honeymoon." In truth, it felt like a honeymoon, a day away from the stress, the planning and whatever was happening up at Royal Lodge HQ.

Instead, she and York had risen with the sunrise streaming through the turret windows, taken the breakfast that magically appeared at their door with a knock and a gloved butler, savored the omelet and croissants, then headed out for a hike up the Highcrest mountain trail to a hillside winery tucked on the far side.

They'd met Stone Ferguson, the brother of Crown Prince John's protection officer, and lunched on a patio overlooking the North Sea.

Then they'd hiked back, strolled hand in hand through town, stopped by the magistrate to sign their marriage license, then shopped and added to their ever-shrinking wardrobe. And spent the night again in the turret.

"Prince Gus said we could use it for the duration of our visit," said York. "And no, I don't know how this happened." He leaned forward, caught her hand. "But I'm not going to argue with favor. I keep thinking about what you said—about God fulfilling the desires of those who fear him."

She rolled her hand over, wove her fingers through his. "And keeping all who love him. Everything is going to be fine, York."

He drew in a breath, withdrew his hand. "I know."

But he didn't. She saw the worry in his eyes.

"Okay, so, it's time for you to tell me what about Ziggy's news had you so freaked out on our wedding day."

He put down his coffee.

"And don't even think about dodging the truth. First, my job is to ferret out secrets." She leaned forward. "And I'm your wife. There are no secrets between us anymore."

His smile was wry. "I see now why you married me."

"I married you for your muscles. But yes, it's just the raw truth now between us, husband."

He smiled. "I like the sound of that word."

"Husband. Me too. Now, spill."

His breath drew in. "Okay, but you won't like it."

"Of course not."

"Whoever killed Gregori left a mark on his body. A circle cut into his chest, with a star in the middle. It's a sort of Russian prison tattoo, but it's come to be the sign of anyone killed by a group called *Oden*. Or roughly translated, the Orphans."

She had finished her waffles, and now picked up her coffee.

"Their leader is ex-Bratva, and the name is specific—they owe no allegiances. And, they trust no one."

"Sounds lonely."

"It makes them impossible to track. They are nameless, faceless and...lethal."

She refused the chill that wanted to ripple through her.

"If an Orphan picked up the contract, then the only way to stop them is to get to the source, have them remove the posting."

"Can Coco just get onto the dark web, find the posting and take it down."

"It comes with a pass code—and not one derived by the user. It's computer generated, impossible to hack and the only way it can be removed is by the owner."

Her mouth tightened. "Is the owner listed on the posting?"

"Not usually. It's all anonymous."

"So, how do we find out who posted it?"

"We fulfill the contract. Get paid, and trace the money back to the source."

She stilled. "York."

"I'm not suggesting we do that." He leaned forward. "But, if anything should happen to me..."

"Nothing is going to happen to you." She put down her coffee. "But it is time to get back to work. We have a ball to prepare for, a director to protect, and a disguise to create."

"And Guilder to frame for it. I'm swamped."

She laughed. Got up and walked over to him. He pushed his chair out and she settled onto his lap, her arms around him. "And if you haven't got your health..."

Then she kissed him.

Yes, she could stay here forever in this fairyland.

Two hours later, however, they sat in Logan Thorne's suite, going over the plans for the evening.

A map lay spread out over the table detailing the ballroom, the doors that lead to the garden, the possible entry points into the ballroom, the balcony locations where Roy and Logan could surveil the dance floor.

The VIP area was right outside the Grand Ballroom in the Grand Hall, where Director Grey would meet the royals in a receiving line. He'd take his mask off there, for the greeting, and everyone would get a good look at him.

Then, he'd move to the ballroom, vanish into the Grand Library next door, and be replaced by York, in the same attire.

York had already died his dark-blond hair a deep-brown, to match, and they'd obtained matching tuxes and masks.

She still had hers from the Shop Vintage, and the golden dress hung in her room at the Royal Lodge.

Ziggy would attend the dance, also, and RJ just felt better knowing Ziggy would be circling the floor.

More assurance that nothing would go wrong.

Logan had already met with the captain of the palace guard, and now Gunner Ferguson had joined them for the final go over. Handsome man, close clipped brown hair, stunning blue eyes, squared jawed, he had a no-nonsense way about him that fit well with York and Roy.

Nothing was going to go wrong tonight.

Meanwhile, she'd done some super sleuthing on the *Oden*, the Orphans, and discovered that the leader York had referred to was a woman.

Ex-KGB spy turned Bratva in the 2000s, she'd left the organization ten years ago after killing a *Pakhan* of the Bratva, one Alexander Latvenko, and vanished. Her name—Raisa Yukachova—surfaced now and again on a number of dark web sites, possible sightings, attributions, even accusations. But no one had seen her, really, in nearly a decade.

It was possible she'd been killed.

But the one thing that identified all Orphans was a tattoo they wore. A circle, with a star in the center, somewhere on their body. A mark of belonging for a group who trusted no one.

Except themselves, it seemed.

Outside, rain began to fall, pinging the windows of the lodge. She looked out at the dark clouds, but beyond them, a blue sky suggested a glorious night for a garden ball.

The others finished their briefing and then she and York left to get ready.

He'd moved into her room in the Royal Lodge, and she tried to fix her hair like Eloise but ended up simply keeping it down.

York zipped her up in the dress, delivered a kiss to the side of her neck, his arms curling around her. "Maybe we should be fashionably late." His voice was a whisper in her ear.

"No. I want to get this over with." She pressed her hands to her stomach, where a knot formed. "I want this to be over so we can go home."

She turned in his arms. "Tell me again about the place you bought?"

"It's on the lake, not far from Jethro's place. A timber home with a wide deck and a gourmet kitchen, two story living room with a giant-stone fireplace, and a master bedroom that overlooks the cascade mountains."

"And extra bedroom for children?"

"Lots of them." He kissed her, sweetly, but she lingered, tasting him, letting the whole of him sweep through her, settle.

Oh, she loved this man. Loved his view of their life.

Longed for it with everything inside her.

She broke away. "Okay, 007. Take me to a ball."

He held out his arm, and she slipped into her golden shoes. "I hope I don't have to run anywhere."

"Me too." He picked up their masks. Hers, with the peacock feather, the gold lace and sequins. His—and Director Grey's—was a simple black silk.

The rain had stopped, the air fresh and clean, the afternoon sun having baked off the water. They joined Logan, Roy and Ziggy—dressed in a black gown, a slit up one side, the skirt slightly flared to hide her ankle holster—and got into a limo provided by Gunner.

Director Grey and his security team were already inside. Marcus and Duncan, both dressed in tuxes, holding their own masks. One would stay with Grey, the other would accompany York.

Grey handed her a transparent earwig. She pressed it into her ear. York did the same.

"We'll turn it on after you get through security," he said.

See. They'd be just fine. And sure, all this security made it harder for anyone to hurt Grey, but frankly, she'd like to be very, very wrong about Grey being a target.

Grey, being York, of course.

The castle courtyard was already full of guests when they arrived, showed their invitations, went through security—or at least the pretense of it. Otis, one of Crown Prince John's men, personally approved them and then they were inside.

York, however, had gone with Otis, donning the uniform of the royal guard, and heading into the castle through a servant's door.

She already missed him.

But Director Grey held out his arm, and RJ looped her gloved hand around his crooked elbow.

"You look beautiful," he said. "And, thank you."

"Glad to do my part."

"Your country—and I—are grateful."

Huh. But it was like York said. She was here to protect the

people around her. Still, a little patriotic pride swelled inside her as they entered the receiving line.

She didn't know if the royals had been briefed or not, but whatever they knew, they betrayed nothing. RJ curtsied for Queen Catherine, dressed in a gorgeous teal blue dress, and King-consort Edric. They greeted her, but turned their attention to Director Grey. In the meantime, RJ directed a curtsy to Princess Gemma and Crown Prince John.

Gemma was resplendent in a creamy-white gown, a feathery neckline with inlaid pearls, her chestnut hair piled up on her head, evidence of Eloise's handiwork. "You look amazing," Princess Gemma said to RJ. "And...how was the wedding?" She gave RJ a conspiratorial smile.

"Perfect," RJ said. "Thank you."

"Is this the bride I heard so much about?" The woman next to Prince Gus looked over at her. Princess Daffy, RJ guessed, with her auburn hair curled and pulled back, wearing an off the shoulder gown with a lace bodice and shimmery green skirt.

"Indeed," Gus said, taking RJ's hand after she curtsied, again. "How was the turret?"

"Breathtaking. Thank you...your highness."

"My pleasure. Anything for a mate of Gunner's."

She glanced over his shoulder where Gunner stood, unblinking, his attention on the crowd. He didn't even look at her.

"Enjoy the ball," Daffy said, then turned to Director Grey for his greeting.

The ballroom was decked out exactly as she would expect—gilded, arched ceiling, white travertine tile, sprays of roses picked fresh from the garden in vases by the open doors.

"I'm a terrible dancer," Grey said as they entered.

"I don't think you'll need to dance." She held up her mask. "Can you tie it on for me?"

It came with silk ties, and the director affixed her, and then she tied on his.

"RJ, can you hear me?" Logan's voice crackled in her ear.

"Copy," she said. Now she felt like a spy.

The room was full, music playing in the background from the full orchestra on stage. "I heard the royals start it out with a quadrille, with a few special guests to form their square. And then, after that, they play dance music—mostly waltzes, maybe a few foxtrots and tangos."

"I'm going to be useless to you."

But York wouldn't. "We should get you to safety."

"RJ, is that you?"

She turned and had nothing at the sight of — "Win? What are you doing here?"

The mask did nothing to hide his face, the handsome jawline, that dark curly hair. "I'm a guest of Princess Gemma. We know each other from our Hollywood days."

Princes Gemma was an actress? But she had no time to follow up because—

"RJ, are you talking to Winchester Marshall?"

This from York, and he didn't sound happy.

"Mmmhmm," she said, still smiling at Win.

"Are you kidding me?"

She hoped Win couldn't hear York huffing in her ear. The actor wore a spiffy gray silk suit, no date on his arm. But, with him was another man, wearing a green mask, a black tux.

"RJ, this is MP Hamish Fickle. He's a member of Lauchtenland's parliament." He turned to Hamish. "This is RJ Marshall, my cousin."

Fickle was a shorter man, but still held a presence. He bowed his head, and he took her hand. "Miss Marshall."

"Actually, it's RJ Newgate now," she said, smiling up at Win.

"That's right it is," York said.

"Really. Well done, Couz. Where is your husband—he's got to be here somewhere." He looked around.

"Watching your every move buddy," York said.

RJ swallowed because she hadn't even thought of Winchester Marshall blowing their cover. "He's...not here." She looked at the Director. "Actually, we have to go."

"Save me a dance?" Winchester asked.

"I'll save you something," York said.

"For Pete's sake," she snapped under her breath, then turned to Win. "Of course." Then she directed Grey away, pushing him toward the library. "I'm not sure what kind of trouble we just got into—or averted, but we need to get this show on the road."

She led him through the costumed crowd. Everyone wore a mask of course, the men in tuxes, the women in glittering gowns.

How was she supposed to spot an assassin in this crowd? *Oh God, keep us*...the thought rose inside her, and she clung to it.

She knocked on the library door, and it opened. Otis and York near the window. "Ready?" York said, tying on his mask.

RJ nodded, and only then did she realize he wasn't talking to her because, "You're a go," Logan responded.

She looked at him. "You going to behave yourself?"

"Probably not." He turned her at the door, met her eyes. "Do not leave me, whatever happens."

"Never."

He kissed her, his hands braced over her shoulders, against the door. Something possessive and every bit the power and taste of York.

Nope, never. "

Then he let her go and extended his arm to her. "Dance?"

"Always and Forever."

The quadrille had started when they emerged from the library, and they stood in the crowd.

RJ tried to scan the crowd, to focus, but she was mesmerized by the movements of the royals—the Queen and her consort, Crown Prince John and Princess Gemma, Prince Gus and Princess Daffy, and another woman, regal in stature, with nearly white-blonde hair, wearing a brilliant red dress, and another man, dark hair, a solemn bearing about him.

"See anyone?" York asked.

Oh. "No. I'm not sure who to look for. Martin? Gustov?"

The crowd applauded their steps.

"That feels like a good start," York said, then pulled her out to the floor as the band started a waltz.

Oh, to be in his arms. But Director Grey wasn't her husband, so she kept a distance between them. He guided her through the waltz, turned her out, back in, moving her perfectly, and though she knew the steps, she surrendered to his lead.

Maybe she was still in the fairytale.

They danced another—a foxtrot—and then he grabbed her hand and headed outside, into the cool air.

Twilight had fallen, the sky a mottled lavender and gold. Beyond the fragrant garden, the smell of the sea lifted. She hadn't walked down to the cliffs to check the fall, but from the turret, it looked treacherous.

"Anybody see anything?" York said now, as he retrieved two glasses of champagne from a waiter. Handed one to RJ.

"Negative. And Otis sent me the list of guests. Everyone has been vetted. Maybe we're in the clear."

Oh, she hoped so.

She would like to enjoy the rest of the evening with her gorgeous husband.

Turning back to the dance, she lifted the champagne to her lips.

Spotted the waiter who'd offered them the glasses.

And something just...clicked. Instincts, maybe, but though the man wore a tuxedo, his hair pulled back in a neat dark man-bun, she saw it.

A circle tattoo, with a center star, right at the nape of his neck.

She whirled and smacked the champagne glass right out York's hand.

It went flying and smashed against a stone planter. He stared at her, stunned.

And maybe so was the waiter, for he turned.

Gotcha.

"The waiter," she said and pointed at the man. "He's *Oden*."

York looked at her glass. Back to the man.

Who dumped his empty tray in a fountain and quickly walked away through the crowd.

"I'll be right back," York said, then took off.

RJ just stood there, holding the champagne glass.

"Ziggy?" Logan said.

"I see him," said Ziggy. "He's escaping through the garden."

Ziggy came into view, hustling in her low heels out through the ballroom, headed after York.

Who had broken out into a run after the man. The waiter hurtled a hedge, knocked over a couple, sending a woman sprawling and made for the cliffs.

Certainly—

RJ still clutched her champagne glass, not sure if it was evidence or not, and started after them.

Get 'em, York.

Ziggy was behind them, running hard, having kicked off her shoes.

The crowd had started to cluster, watching the chaos.

A few more palace security had arrived, also running hard, some shouting.

"RJ." A voice behind her turned, and it was Roy. He stood behind her, and it hit her that she was Roy's assignment, if something should go down.

Oh, York.

He'd caught up to the man, and a couple women had gasped as he tackled the man, scrubbing him onto the ground.

But the man rolled, punched York and while she winced, some of the women turned away.

Ziggy was hard on his tail even as York caught the man with his leg and dumped him off him. RJ couldn't tell if he was bleeding—probably, but he bounced up and just barely dodged another punch.

York had his feet about him, though, and waiter wasn't going to last long. Not with Ziggy twenty yards away, and a cadre of palace staff behind her.

The sun was just winking out, a glorious orange haze over the far away purple horizon, a cluster of red caught in the clouds as York launched himself at the waiter.

And then...

Oh...*what—?*

The scream burbled up even as others gasped, as screams and shouts of horror lifted.

RJ's knees buckled, and she would have dropped except for Roy's arms around her.

He didn't—he hadn't—

But as Ziggy ran up to the edge of the cliff, looking over, as she turned, her hand over her mouth, turning back to them in a thousand-yard stare, the truth hit RJ like a poison, flushing into her bones, shuddering through her, and then flushing out of her in a full out, body-shaking scream.

York had gone over the side of the cliff.

"No. No—no —"

Roy's arms tightened around her, even as he spoke into the comms. "Ziggy. Report —"

From the bank, she shook her head.

More castle guards appeared, stood at the edge. Some backed away.

"Ziggy?"

"Take RJ off comms," Ziggy said softly.

No—no— RJ pushed against Roy, met his eyes.

He let her go.

Then she was up, running hard, kicking off her golden shoes, running barefoot through the garden, onto the grasses, her heart out of her body, even as Roy ran behind her.

Ziggy caught her before she reached the edge— "No, RJ—"

But she tore through Ziggy's grasp, pushing her way to the edge.

Roy grabbed her around the waist with his good arm, maybe to keep her from going over the edge.

Probably the right move because right then, with everything inside her, she would have. Simply launched herself off the edge in a terrible, wretched grief-stricken act just so she could join the body laying a hundred feet below, at the bottom of the cliffs, wrecked among the waves as they slammed against the rock.

She stood there watching, unable to breathe, unable to think as the waves swept up the body, drew it out, and then, she fell to her knees as it sank under the froth of the sea.

And right then, the sun fell into the darkness, leaving only the bruised sky and the terrible, tragic end of the fairytale.

What Happens Next?

Chapter 20/Portami a casa: un ricordo della resistenza italiana

I don't blame Bertie. How can I—he is five, and he doesn't know the terrible truth of his actions.

Besides, how can I blame a child for the workings of the Almighty?

I can hear Fred, his soft, low voice as he says, shall we not accept good from the Lord, and not trouble? May the name of the Lord be praised.

I cling to that now, along with the memory of my husband in the glow of the morning light as he kneels by the window, praying, his head bowed, and I realize anew that he has given me something greater than love.

He has returned to me faith. Hope.

The truth that God watches my life.

He will fulfill the desires of the man who fears him.

Even if I do not understand how.

It happened so fast, it has taken months for me to unravel it, to see it clearly.

To find my footing against the grief that would undo me.

Too easily I can close my eyes and hear the voices, the Panzer unit that enters the front gate of the monastery.

The monks simply let them in. They claimed to be bearing gifts for the Abbey, but I believe that Father Cantero lets them in to give us time.

To alert all those harboring within the walls to hide, or perhaps run.

And perhaps, if he is amiable, they will not search for us.

Still, I am shattered, unable to speak as the Waffen-SS drive into the yard, disembark from their vehicles.

The shouting in German begins almost immediately, the ruse broken as soldiers invade the yard, search the buildings.

I am standing in the kitchen, packing our bags for the journey that will take us to the border, to join Fred's unit. He is still MIA, but he assures me that we will be safe.

I believe him. And not because we will not be found, or executed, but I have realized that safety is not a word meant for earth. It is a state of being. A perspective of the eternal.

The monks are rubbing off on me, perhaps.

In this moment, however, I have no perspective except fear.

If not for Fred, I would yet be in the kitchen, holding our travel food so generously offered by the monks. He arrived, grabbed me up and tore me from my fear into action. We dared not secret ourselves back to our chamber, but instead he led us along the corridors, towards the church, where there is an entrance out of the north transept. I supposed he meant for us to run into the hills and hide, like before.

Certainly, the soldiers will respect the sacred ground of the church.

We reach the Sacristy, and then horror fills my throat. Through an arched window in the yard, I spot Bertie and Arturo. They are picking up goods from the monastery for locals—honey, bread, jams—and most importantly, travelers.

Today, those travelers include—and I can barely breathe it—Tory and a group of resistance fighters, his young friends who have been hiding here, it seems. They are caught on the night stairs from the upstairs dorter, probably on their way out, into the nave and the north church transept.

So far, hidden, but it won't be long before the Germans find them.

I squeeze Fred's hand and point, and he stops.

The brothers are loading the horse-drawn cart. Bertie is playing in the dirt with a stick, oblivious to the terror upon us.

We could keep running. There is nothing between us and the transept, us and freedom.

But for Tory, trapped at the top of the stairs, I would. But he is my brother.

And Fred knows this.

"There is another stairs," Fred says softly. "It leads to the south transept. I'll get them."

I'll get them. But what can I say?

Fred leans down, touches my face with his hand, then kisses me. Quick. Sure.

Always and Forever.

He is gone before I can protest, but I wouldn't. Instead, I watch as Fred climbs the stairs to the dorter, and I pray.

In the yard, Germans have arrived to search the cart, but of course, there is not one—praise be to small miracles. Tory and his two friends have receded to the shadows.

And then it happens. A sound perhaps, but Bertie looks up the stairs. Lifts his hand to wave.

No one has seen him yet, but I know he is greeting Tory.

I act without thought, impulse, or panic. Some might call it courage, but I can only do the right thing, that truth that burns through me.

"Bertie!"

I push out of the door into the courtyard.

Everyone turns. Arturo, who is standing by the cart, Bertie, the Germans.

"Angelica!" He runs towards me, and I kneel in front of him.

And then a chill freezes me as I hear my name, growled out with a German accent.

I look up as a shadow crosses me.

Obergruppenfuehrer Heinlein.

He reaches out, grabs me up by the arm. Leans in close. "I knew I would find you."

And now I know. I have brought disaster to this place. More importantly, I have killed my brother.

I know then that it is too late for me and something akin to fury possesses me. How dare they bring evil to this place, to our lives?

I yank my arm away from him, push him back and of course, this only inflames him.

But what will he do to me, here, in this sacred place?

And I am right. He pulls his hand back, as if to hit me, and Father Cantero lets out a shout.

It stops Heinlein who lowers his hand, nearly shaking.

I dare not glance at the stairs, dare not give away Fred and Tory.

Please, be safe.

I am led away to the yard and I don't look back.

He puts me in his car, in the front seat, but I refuse to tremble.

And I pray that Fred will run.

But I know he will not.

Shouting lifts behind me, and I want to close my eyes as soldiers haul out their finds—Jews and a handful of partisans hiding in the Sacristy.

None of them are Tory. Or Fred.

Still, my relief is short-lived as they are all—to a one, including women and children—lined up and shot.

The sound still echoes in my soul.

Father Cantero, five other monks, and six lay brothers are taken as the SS rolls out of the yard.

Heinlein drives me straight to my home. It is quiet. Empty.

And I am terrified.

He drags me from the car, because my legs have stopped working. Pushes me into the house.

I will not let him have me.

And yes, for Fred, I must live.

The kitchen pan is where it fell in the kitchen, and swoop it up, my defense against Heinlein as he pursues me. Out of the kitchen, into the yard. I am weeping, furious, terrified—

And then I see him. A dark, furious, resolved hero, running from the courtyard, straight at Heinlein.

He has justice on his countenance as he takes down the German. I can't watch, but I can't stop myself.

Please.

Heinlein, for all his presence, is no match for a man whose wife has been threatened.

I turn away, however, when Fred gets Heinlein's gun and fires.

The report echoes into the air and shakes through me.

Then, Fred's arms are around me, pulling me tight against him. He is bloody, and sweaty and shaking and yet he holds me up.

I am still in his arms when the rest of Heinlein's escort pulls up.

Despite his hand in mine, pulling me across the yard, toward the grotto, we are found.

Gunfire, and Fred grabs me, pulls me to the ground, his body over mine.

It jerks with the fire, and I know, even as he holds me, the truth.

"Always and Forever," he says when the shooting stops.

I lay there, under weight of his embrace, even when I hear more shouts, more gunfire.

More death.

I lay there, willing Fred to breathe, his heart to beat again, willing him to stay.

Faint is the memory of Tory easing Fred off me, of taking me in his arms. Faint is the memory of the next days, even weeks where he hides me in the grotto, back where the Janowitzes *lived.*

Faint is the memory of the Allies, pushing into Lucca, pushing back the invaders just three months later.

By that time, Sigfrid is alive inside me, kicking, and that memory is vivid. Shall we not accept good from the Lord, and not trouble?

Sigfrid is born in the early hours of June 2, 1945, one month after the surrender of the German forces. He has Fred's eyes—golden-brown, and in them I see Fred's wisdom.

And I hold in my arms hope. Love. Joy.

As I tend my vines, pray for this land, I sometimes hear Fred's voice, low and deep and in my bones, or on the hush of the wind. The Lord is near to those who call on him. He fulfills the desires of those who fear him.

Always and Forever.

RJ closed her eyes, even as she closed the book. Pulled it to her chest even as she worried the rings on her finger and stared out to the cliffs of Lauchtenland. Rain pattered the roof, its breath thick upon the air but here, under the roof of the deck of the Royal Lodge, sitting on an Adirondack chair, she was dry.

If not cold.

But she'd been cold for the better part of a week as the Lauchtenland Rescue searched for York's body.

The man on the rocks, the one she'd seen engulfed by the

waves belonged to Sergio Komarov, former member of the Bratva, currently known under a dozen aliases, wanted by Interpol for more murders than she wanted to know.

And definitely a member of the Orphans.

She'd asked Gunner to sit on that information for a while...

Because she had a plan.

"Hey, we're getting ready to go. Are you packed?" Ziggy came out of the door of the lodge.

RJ handed her the book. "Thank you."

Ziggy took it. "So?"

"It's amazing."

"Sad."

"But also real. It's the way of life, really. And I suppose the only way to get through this—to remember that God is near to us."

Ziggy clutched the book to herself. "Yes." She drew in a breath, met RJ's gaze. "I lost someone I loved terribly also, and it's not the same—we weren't married—but it still gutted me."

RJ stared at her, nonplussed. Ziggy was always so buttoned up, so...capable. RJ couldn't imagine her gutted.

"It does get easier."

"York's not dead." RJ got up. "I've been down this road with him. He's not dead. And I'm not going anywhere quite yet."

"RJ —"

She stopped in front of Ziggy, especially when Roy came out of the door. Held up her hand. "I know it sounds crazy, but...right before York...faked his death, he told me about how to figure out who posted the bounty." She waited until Roy joined Ziggy. "We confirm the kill—and I know we can get Coco to make that happen. Witnesses of him going over the cliff, and shots of the waiter we pulled out of the water—she can manipulate it, put York's face on it —"

"RJ —"

"It will work." She refused to raise her voice, instead took a breath and turned it low. "I've been over and over this, looking at the trajectories, the angles, the what-ifs—York survived that fall. I know it in my bones. And now he wants me to confirm his death and follow the money trail when the assassin gets paid."

Ziggy raised an eyebrow, her mouth a grim line. But she nodded.

Roy cupped his good hand behind his neck, kneaded a muscle there.

"It's worth a try. Even if he's..." Her eyes burned but she blinked the moisture away. "Even if I'm wrong, we find the person who..."

"Who is behind his murder," Ziggy said quietly.

RJ looked away.

The sky was still mottled and gray from the storm, although it had started to die, and through a fissure in the clouds, the sun had broken through. The air smelled of summer, and in that heartbeat, she was in the turret, the wind playing with the curtains at the windows, York in her arms, his breath in her ear.

"We will live happily ever after, RJ. Trust me."

She did trust him.

And he trusted her.

"Are you with me, or do I have to do this alone?"

Ziggy considered her. Then smiled and held out her fist.

Roy sighed. But also held his out.

She bumped them both. "Good. Because this story isn't over. Not by a long shot. Now, I'm going to need some fresh coffee."

Continue the adventure!

NO MATTER THE COST

The worst has happened—but RJ refuses to believe it, and until she has proof, she's going to keep searching for answers.

But the past won't stay quiet, and it'll take a trip back to

Russia, to York's past to find the answers that will save lives...the kind of answers that dig up the secrets and lies that have embedded York's life.

And even then, does RJ have what it takes—with, or without the man she loves—to save the world from Martin's terrible plan?

The riveting conclusion to the epic adventure of RJ and York!

A NOTE FROM SUSIE MAY

Thank you so much for reading ***I Will Find You!*** I hope you enjoyed the story. If you did, would you be willing to do me a favor? Head over to the **product page** and leave a review. It doesn't have to be long—just a few words to help other readers know what they're getting. (But no spoilers! We don't want to wreck the fun!)

I'd love to hear from you—not only about this story, but about any characters or stories you'd like to read in the future. Write to me at: susan@susanmaywarren.com.

I also have a monthly update that contains sneak peeks, reviews, upcoming releases, and free, fun stuff for my reader friends. Sign up at www.susanmaywarren.com

And, if you're interested reading more epic romantic suspense, head over to https://www.susanmaywarren.com/genre/contemporary-romantic-suspense/

Thank you again for reading!

Susie May

About Susan May Warren

With over 1.5 million books sold, critically acclaimed novelist Susan May Warren is the Christy, RITA, and Carol award-winning author of over forty-five novels with Tyndale, Barbour, Steeple Hill, and Summerside Press. Known for her compelling plots and unforgettable characters, Susan has written contemporary and historical romances, romantic-suspense, thrillers, rom-com, and Christmas novellas.

With books translated into eight languages, many of her novels have been ECPA and CBA bestsellers, were chosen as Top Picks by *Romantic Times*, and have won the RWA's Inspirational Reader's Choice contest and the American Christian Fiction Writers Book of the Year award. She's a three-time RITA finalist and an eight-time Christy finalist.

Publishers Weekly has written of her books, "Warren lays bare her characters' human frailties, including fear, grief, and resentment, as openly as she details their virtues of love, devotion, and resiliency. She has crafted an engaging tale of romance, rivalry, and the power of forgiveness."

Library Journal adds, "Warren's characters are well-developed and she knows how to create a first rate contemporary romance..."

Susan is also a nationally acclaimed writing coach, teaching at conferences around the nation, and winner of the 2009 American Christian Fiction Writers Mentor of the Year award. She loves to help people launch their writing careers. She is the founder of www.MyBookTherapy.com and www.LearnHowtoWriteaNovel.com, a writing website that helps authors get published and stay published. She is also the author of the popular writing method *The Story Equation.*

Find excerpts and reviews of her novels at www.susanmaywarren.com and connect with her on social media.

facebook.com/susanmaywarrenfiction
instagram.com/susanmaywarren
twitter.com/susanmaywarren
bookbub.com/authors/susan-may-warren
goodreads.com/susanmaywarren
amazon.com/Susan-May-Warren

CONTINUE THE ADVENTURE

THE EPIC STORY OF RJ AND YORK

Book 1: Out of the Night

Book 2: I Will Find You

Book 3: No Matter the Cost

Also by Susan May Warren

FIND OTHER EPIC ROMANTIC ADVENTURES BY SMW!

Sky King Ranch

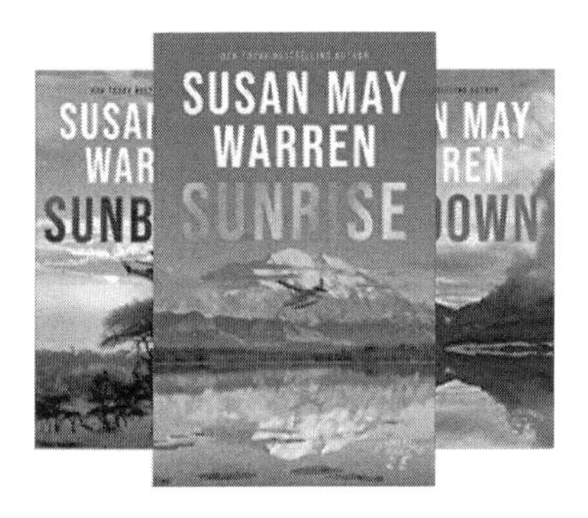

Global Search and Rescue

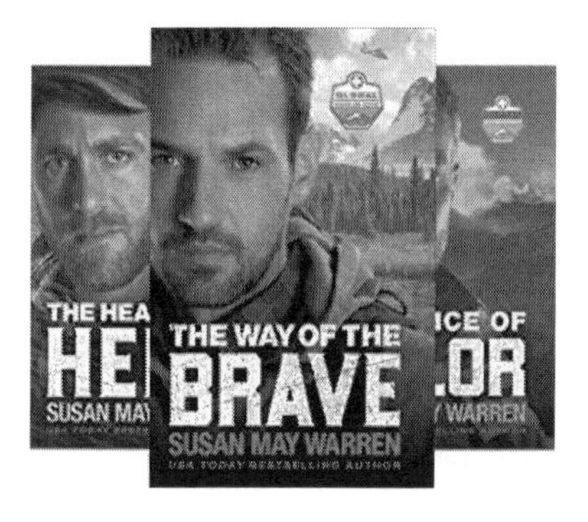

The Montana Marshalls

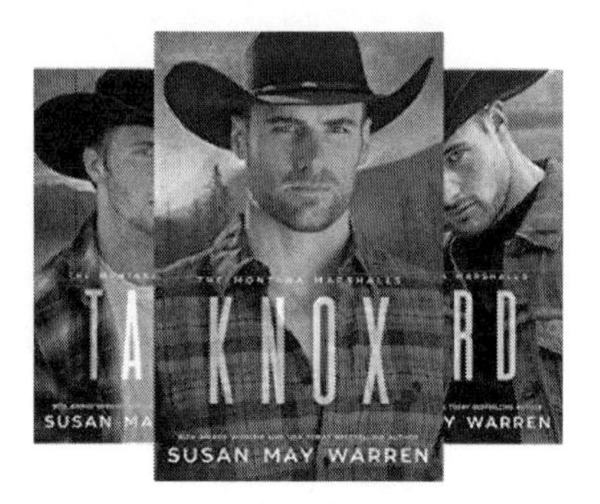

Montana Rescue

Montana Fire

Global Guardians

I Will Find You

The Epic Story of RJ and York series

Published by SDG Publishing

15100 Mckenzie Blvd. Minnetonka, MN 55345

This book is a work of fiction. Names, characters, places, and incidents are either products of the author's imagination or used fictitiously. Any similarity to actual people, organizations, and/or events is purely coincidental.

Scripture quotations are taken from the King James Version of the Bible.

For more information about Susan May Warren, please access the author's website at the following address: www.susanmaywarren.com.

Published in the United States of America.

Made in the USA
Middletown, DE
11 April 2023